GAZILLIONS OF REPTILIANS

FREAKY FLORIDA BOOK 7

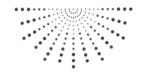

WARD PARKER

MAD MANGROVE MEDIA

ISBN: 978-1-7345511-8-1

CONTENTS

THE DEAD UNDEAD

On the night they found Marvin's remains, Missy was removing plaque from a vampire's fangs.

"I never knew you also did dental work," Mrs. Kinkuddy said.

"Just the basics," Missy said. "You'll have to get a home health dentist here for an extraction or something serious. Open wider. How often do you brush your fangs?"

"Oh, I try to do it every morning before I go to bed."

"Turn your head a bit more toward me. The good thing about being on a liquid diet is you don't need to floss as often. But you do need to brush regularly, Mrs. Kinkuddy. You wouldn't want to have a fang pulled, would you?"

"Uh-uhn," her patient replied awkwardly as Missy scraped away plaque. Missy had to be careful with her fingers in the mouth of a vampire. The instinct to sink their fangs into flesh was hard for the creatures to resist.

Many of Missy's patients no longer hunted, though. They

fed upon bags of blood from the daily Blood Bus, donated by unsuspecting people who thought their blood was going to help some poor human in a hospital. Many of her patients still had dentures they had worn as humans before being turned into vampires. The long, sharp canine teeth came with their new condition. The rest of their teeth, or lack thereof, remained the same.

Missy was just finishing sharpening her patient's fangs when a commotion arose in the hallway.

"Wonder wha at ith?" Mrs. Kinkuddy asked.

Loud knocks struck the door.

"Excuse me, dear," Mrs. Kinkuddy said, racing to the door almost quicker than the eye, like a vampire decades younger.

A bunch of elderly Squid Tower vampires stood in the hall. All were agitated.

"Marvin's dead!" said Bill, a member of Missy's vampire writing group.

"Marvin Nutley?" Mrs. Kinkuddy asked.

"Yes! The only Marvin on our floor. He's my next-door neighbor, and I hadn't seen or heard him in two nights. So, I stuck my head around the wall of my balcony and saw him sitting out on his. Dead. Sun-torched."

"Oh, my," Missy and Mrs. Kinkuddy said at the same time.

"I think he fell asleep in his chair one night, and the rising sun got him."

"Impossible," an elderly vampire in the hall said. "The pain from the first exposure to the sun would have awakened him and allowed him to get inside before he was torched."

"Has anyone called Agnes?" Missy asked about the HOA president and leader of the community.

"I did," said Bill, who was also on the HOA board. He liked

to pretend he'd been in the military, acting with dispassionate efficiency in everything he did. The truth was, he'd never worn a uniform in his life or afterlife, except as a costume when playing soldier with his extensive weapons collection.

"Agnes is here." The words rippled through the crowd in the hallway. Missy and her patient joined them as they followed Agnes, striding with her quad cane, from the elevator to 409. The petite ninety-year-old (in body age), wore a grim expression as she unlocked the door with a spare key.

When she walked in, the crowd held back, despite their curiosity. Being a nurse, Missy decided she should follow Agnes. They walked through the sparsely furnished two-bedroom apartment. Marvin was a notorious cheapskate who had claimed he needed to nurse his modest savings to last him for eternity. The rumor, though, was he was actually filthy rich. You wouldn't know it from the thrift-store furnishings in his living room.

When they reached the sliding glass door to the balcony, Agnes yanked on the handle and gasped with surprise.

"It's locked," she said. "How could it be locked if he was out there?"

"Murder."

Missy jumped in surprise. She hadn't realized Mrs. Kinkuddy was standing right behind them.

"Someone locked Marvin out there and let him fry."

"But surely, he would have called for help," Agnes said. "You're his neighbor, Bill. You didn't hear anything?"

"No," Bill replied. "I rarely go on my balcony unless I'm watching out for human-smugglers landing on the beach. I don't think I'd hear him shouting if I was inside. The question is, did anyone else hear him and ignore it?"

"You mean, ignore it even while knowing the sunrise was coming?" Missy asked.

Bill shrugged. "I'm just saying."

"Let's not speak ill of the dead undead," Agnes said. "I wish I hadn't touched the handle. We'll need to get a security firm to check it for fingerprints."

Missy, still wearing her latex gloves from the dental exam, unlatched the door and slid it open. The three of them stepped hesitantly onto the balcony. There was no need to turn on the light, since Missy could see well enough in the moonlight, and the vampires could see even better. The space was small, with room for a glass-top table, two chairs, and a sun lounger.

Ironically, the sun lounger was where the black husk of what used to be Marvin Nutley lay. It looked like one of the volcanic-ash-preserved corpses from the ruins of Pompeii.

"He looks almost peaceful lying there," Agnes said. "I want to believe he didn't suffer too much."

A gust of wind from the ocean hit Marvin's blackened remains and blasted the ashes all over the three of them and onto nearby balconies. Nothing was left of Marvin but a small pile of ashes in the corner and a coating on the cushion of the sun lounger. Missy wiped ashes from her face.

"There goes my plan of filling an urn with what was left of Marvin," Agnes said.

When you're a vampire, your hive or greater community must be completely self-sufficient, because many of the services you need can't be supplied by humans. Undead patients can't go to human doctors, so they contract with home health agencies like Missy's. In the rare event that one of you expires, you can't turn to a funeral home.

And, in the case of crime, you have to investigate it yourself, except, perhaps, for simple burglaries or car thefts. You really don't want the police involved in your affairs. You can't take any risk of them finding out you're vampires.

That is especially true in the event of vampicide, the killing of a vampire by another vampire or a human. Agnes and her associates would have to find the killer and mete out justice.

Missy was determined to help, though. She was the community's most-trusted human, almost like an honorary vampire. The only other humans the community dealt with were those they hired to do landscaping, maintenance, guarding the gate, and other daytime activities. The association's attorney happened to be a werewolf, but he could work during the day, obviously.

"I'm calling an emergency meeting of the Board of Directors," Agnes said. "Assuming no one is out and about hunting prey, we'll meet downstairs in an hour."

"WHO CARES WHO KILLED HIM?" asked Leonard Schwartz at the Squid Towers HOA Board of Directors emergency meeting.

The other four members gasped at his insensitivity. Missy, sitting in an empty row of folding chairs across from them, wisely kept her mouth shut.

"I know you don't have a drop of compassion in your undead body," Agnes said, "but the association bylaws forbid killing anyone on the property."

"I thought that meant no feeding on humans."

"It means humans, vampires, or any other sentient advanced creature. We are a self-governing community. If we don't follow the rules, we'll descend into anarchy."

Schwartz snorted with derision.

"Don't you snort at me," Agnes said. "The only killing allowed in our community is when we must put a vampire to final death as punishment for serious offenses. Like killing a neighbor."

"You executed a vampire years ago for putting unauthorized holiday decorations on her front door," Kim said.

"Exactly. Serious offenses like that."

"Agnes, you know as well as I do Marvin antagonized half the community with his crazy conspiracy theories," Schwartz said.

"They're not all crazy," Bill said.

"Yeah, the ones you believe in, too, aren't crazy," Gloria said. "I get it."

"All I'm saying is that finding and punishing whoever locked him out on his balcony will be very divisive for our community," Schwartz said.

"You mean it's permissible to murder unpopular residents?" Agnes asked. "If that's the case, you'd better watch your back."

Schwartz snorted again. "No one at Squid Towers has the guts to take me on. That includes you, Bill. I mean fighting me fang to fang, not shooting me with wooden bullets from half a mile away with one of your sniper rifles."

"Okay, turn the testosterone down, boys," Kim said.

"At a hundred and seventy-five years old, I still have testosterone?"

"I know I do," Bill said. "Considerably more than you."

"You're going to cause a lot of anger if you go around asking people who disliked Marvin, of whom there are many, if they murdered him," Gloria said.

"I don't see what other option we have," Agnes said. "Any of us could become victims of casual murder if we allow this to go unpunished."

"So, we have to question everyone?" Gloria asked.

"Unless there's a better option," Agnes said, fixing Missy with her stare. "Such as magic."

"Wait a minute, I'm a nurse here," Missy said. "I need to maintain the trust of my patients. I can't do that if I'm a witch-inquisitor."

"No one has to know," Agnes said. "You simply help us narrow down the suspects. We'll take it from there."

"I don't know of any spells powerful enough to find the killer out of all the residents here. All I have is a truth-telling spell. And I have to use that face-to-face with the subject. I won't do that."

"Do browse through your spell books and see if you can find one that will help us, please," Agnes said.

"Okay," Missy said, though she had no intention of doing so. "But you guys can do a little more to narrow down the half of the population who disliked him without interrogating every-one. Do you know of any quarrels he's had recently? Has anyone threatened him? Complained about him behind his back?"

"Those who complained about him behind his back make up the half of us who disliked him," Kim said.

"Well, you know what I mean. There have to be some suspects who come to mind first."

"Bill, here, wasn't too fond of him," Schwartz said.

"Hey, I'm the one who found him. I was concerned about his wellbeing. He didn't answer his door, so I looked around the wall into his balcony. Speaking of fondness, I saw you yelling at him after he parked in the handicapped spot you claim as your own."

"It *is* mine," Schwartz said. "And I'm not the only one here prone to yelling at Marvin. Kim, if I recall, screamed at him at the pool just last week."

"He was going on loudly with the new vampire couple from Scranton about his latest conspiracy theory. He was so loud and obnoxious, not one of us could hear the pool aerobics instructor."

"And Gloria, you've been quiet tonight," Schwartz taunted. "But you're not innocent. I heard you rip into him when he accused you of being a Reptilian."

"Of course, I did," she said. "How can a vampire be a Reptilian?"

"But can a Reptilian be a vampire? That's where he was coming from."

"It's utterly idiotic," Gloria said. "And insulting. How dare he accuse me of that!"

"What's a Reptilian?" Missy asked.

They all ignored her.

"Marvin had an entire insane asylum's worth of conspiracy theories in his head," Agnes said. "But the lizard-people one has to be the craziest."

"Lizard people?" Missy asked.

"I thought you young people knew everything on the internet," Schwartz said.

"I'm not so young. And I don't read conspiracy theories on the internet."

"Maybe you should start. If you want to understand Marvin's mind."

She did not want to understand Marvin's mind. He wasn't a

patient of hers, but she'd met him and knew he was a kook. An abrasive kook. But she supposed if she was going to help the people of Squid Tower find justice without making themselves devolve into a civil war, she should find out more of why Marvin antagonized all his neighbors. She had the following night off and would do some research.

What she learned about Marvin's world turned her reality-based world completely upside down.

Missy leafed through a few of her grimoires. She called them her magick recipe books. They contained advice and instructions for everything from spells to potions, from hexes to amulets. There was magick to heal warts and inspire love. There were spells to make your fields yield more crops and your 401K yield more earnings.

But she didn't find any spells for finding murder suspects. She didn't expect to. And really didn't want to. She worried about making a mistake and falsely accusing a Squid Tower resident. Besides, she wanted to use her magick to help others, not for law enforcement.

Instead, she turned to the internet. The internet was useless for finding spells that actually worked. Those were extremely valuable, so why would you post them on the internet for free?

The internet was more suitable for finding wacky conspiracy theories. After all, wasn't that what the internet was invented for?

It didn't take long to find Marvin Nutley's extensive internet presence. It turned out he was a prolific writer of screeds defending his outlandish conspiracy theories and attacking his critics.

Most of his work were videos in which he laid out the case that the moon landing was faked, Elvis was still alive, and Bigfoot was holding Elvis prisoner in a cabin in the woods. The contrails in the sky from jets were chemicals that made us more docile. Moreover, the earth was flat. Every manmade tragedy was a false-flag operation, and everything that happened in the world was part of an evil plot by a secret cabal.

Many of his videos were Marvin talking to the camera about Reptilians, also known as Lizard People. These aliens from another solar system could shape-shift into human form and blend into our society. In fact, many of the most powerful individuals on the planet—in politics, business, and culture— were, in fact, Reptilians. Soon, they would completely run the world and enslave all the humanoids through mind control.

He used a lot of obscure, impossible-to-verify proof points and anecdotes to prove his theory. But mostly he talked about it as if it didn't need to be proven, as if it was common knowledge accepted by everyone.

It was nuts. It would have been funny if Marvin wasn't so vehement about it.

Missy found videos from other conspiracy theorists who believed in Reptilians. Marvin wasn't the only one out there. But he was most likely the only vampire purveyor of the Reptilian conspiracy. That was a distinction he was surely proud of before he was incinerated.

Marvin had been in his sixties in body age, the age when he was turned into a vampire. Missy didn't know how long ago that was. It was impressive enough that a guy in his sixties had mastered the internet propaganda channels. For a guy probably more than a century old, it was remarkable.

Missy, in her forties, didn't even know how to make a video of herself and post it on the internet. How lame was that?

So far, what Missy found confirmed Marvin was as far off the deep end as his neighbors claimed. But it didn't provide clues as to why he was killed.

Those took a little longer to find.

She found them in a video titled, "Video proof that Reptilians Exist." Intriguing, yes. Who wouldn't watch this video?

This one wasn't like the others, with Marvin at home lecturing to his laptop camera. He shot this video with his smartphone in some rural location. He spoke breathlessly to the jerky camera.

"I'm here at the edge of the Florida Everglades. This area is well-known as a landing site for Reptilians arriving here from the Alpha Draconis star system. Their spaceships are invisible to humans, of course. But burn marks have been found on the grounds of a nearby campground that were made by the spaceship engines. And—hey, why is there a man walking by in the middle of the night in such a remote area?"

Sure enough, there was movement far in the background behind Marvin's face. He turned the camera to face whatever moved. After the camera adjusted to the moonlight, it focused on a man walking.

Marvin zoomed in. Yes, it definitely was a man. And he was naked.

Oh no, Missy thought. Is this going to be yet another drunk, naked Florida Man story?

"See how tall the man is?" Marvin whispered excitedly. "He

has a good probability of being a Reptilian. Not just the height, but the fact he is naked. He has shed his humanoid clothing."

The camera jerked but remained on the naked man.

"I have to be careful to remain unseen. I don't want to be eaten by the Reptilian."

Missy didn't want to see him confronted by a drunk, naked Florida Man.

But then, the impossible happened.

The man shape-shifted.

It happened so quickly and smoothly that it seemed perfectly natural. The walking man transformed into a giant dragon.

Yes, a dragon walking on four legs with a lengthy tail, folded wings on its back, and spikes on its sinuous neck.

The dragon turned its head and saw Marvin.

"Oh boy, oh boy, he's seen me. He's going to kill me. I need to do something."

Actually, the dragon looked more curious than ready to attack. It was probably just as surprised to see Marvin as Marvin was seeing him.

With the camera still trained on the dragon, Marvin's other hand appeared in the frame. It was holding a handgun.

Oh, my, Missy thought. That's not a good idea.

Two loud bangs with the camera jerking. Muzzle flashes from the gun.

The dragon flinched as it was hit.

By all rights, Marvin should be done for. He never should have survived to meet his demise in a sun lounger on his balcony. The dragon should have torched him with its fiery breath or chomped him in half with its giant jaws right then and there.

But instead, the dragon unfolded huge, sail-like wings that flapped mighty strokes and lifted it into the air. Marvin took another shot at it as it disappeared into the night sky.

"I did it! I finally did it!" Marvin screamed into the camera, which was way too close to his fat face. "I got proof they exist! Reptilians exist!"

It hadn't convinced Missy. What was caught on video wasn't a Reptilian from outer space. It was just a dragon. Missy had seen her share of dragons before. She hadn't known they could shape-shift, but that was clearly the case.

But what freaked her out was the dragon looked familiar. Even in the bad lighting, she recognized its distinct brown-green coloring, the shape of its head, the missing tip of one of its head horns.

She knew this dragon. It was Ronnie, whom she had found in the Everglades, when he was an injured juvenile, and nursed back to health.

Ronnie had learned he was destined to be a king of the dragons. And Marvin had shot him.

Maybe it wasn't the sunlight that had incinerated Marvin on his balcony after all.

2

WELCOME TO MY CONSPIRACY THEORY

O bviously, Marvin survived his foolhardy shooting of Ronnie. Initially. He was alive to post the video, and his immolated body was found a week after the posting date.

Missy was surprised at Ronnie's restraint. Dragons aren't known as easy-come, easy-go creatures. By all rights, Marvin should have been incinerated. Or, perhaps, torn to pieces and then incinerated.

But did Ronnie track Marvin down and finish the job a week later? Missy hadn't seen any peripheral burn marks on the balcony, but she didn't know how pinpointed a dragon's fiery breath could be.

She needed to contact Ronnie, partly to find out if he was the culprit. That would save any residents of Squid Tower from being falsely accused of Marvin's murder.

Also, she wanted to make sure Ronnie was okay after being shot. She'd grown fond of the talking dragon since she first found him years ago.

The only way she knew to call Ronnie was to communicate telepathically with him. She didn't have the ability, but he did, and they had communicated this way before.

Ronnie, this is Missy. Can you hear me? she asked in her head.

After repeating the line several times, she tried saying it aloud. Again, and again.

Soon, her two gray tabby cats gathered around and stared at her quizzically.

"No, I'm not crazy. I'm just trying to contact a dragon. Which sounds insane in its own right."

Eventually, she gave up. The best she could hope for was that Ronnie's consciousness had been tickled by her thoughts.

SHE MADE the decision to tell only Agnes about Marvin's dragon video. All supernatural creatures need to keep their existence secret from humans as best they can, which was especially the case for dragons. After all, they had nearly been wiped off the face of the earth by humans centuries ago. Obviously, dragons couldn't fit anonymously into society like vampires and werewolves. Ronnie's shape-shifting was the only example she knew of dragons having the ability to do that.

Otherwise, the giant beasts had to hide in the Everglades or in the vast impenetrable forests that remained in the world. Most dragons regularly travelled to the alternate plane of existence called the In Between to find sanctuary.

"He shot the dragon?" Agnes asked in disbelief.

Missy nodded. "You want to see the video?"

"I suppose I must."

15

Missy played it for the 1,500-year-old vampire on her laptop in the card room where residents played canasta and bridge three days a week.

After Marvin's shots rang out, Agnes shook her head.

"What kind of idiot would shoot at a dragon?" she asked. "Do you suppose the dragon found him on his balcony?"

"Possibly. But I would have expected to see more burn damage to the balcony and the other furniture. And it doesn't explain why the door was locked from the inside."

"I hope this video doesn't get around. We have too many hotheads living here who could cause trouble."

"The video has only had a few dozen views," Missy said. "Let's hope it stays undiscovered."

Bill, Oleg, and Sol burst into the room.

"Have you seen Marvin's video?" Bill asked excitedly. "He shot a shape-shifting Reptilian!"

Missy groaned inwardly.

"It looked like a dragon to me," Sol said.

"What's the difference? It's a Reptilian."

"I thought you didn't believe in that nonsense," Oleg said in his Russian accent.

"I do now. You saw the video. Don't you believe?"

"It was a dragon," Sol said.

"A reptile is a reptile is a Reptilian, here to take over the world through mind control. We have to fight back."

"Why?" Missy asked.

"It's obvious the Reptilian killed Marvin," Bill said. "It was wounded and enraged. It tracked him down while in dragon form and burned him to death with its fiery breath."

"Let me put this to rest," Missy said. "I recognize that dragon. I nursed him back to health when he was young and had a broken wing. His name is Ronnie, and he was prophesied to one day be the king of all the dragons. Apparently, when he matured, he developed the ability to shape-shift. So, he's not some Reptilian from outer space. He's Ronnie from Gainesville, Florida. And he was a nice guy, for a dragon."

"He murdered our friend Marvin," Bill said.

"First of all, we don't know he murdered Marvin. Second, Marvin wasn't your friend. You complained about him all the time."

"As a fellow vampire, I'm on his side against the Reptilian invaders."

"It sounds unlikely that a dragon torched Marvin on his balcony," Agnes said. "Surely, someone would have seen a dragon hovering outside our building. And how would the dragon have known which condo was Marvin's and that he would be out on his balcony at that time?"

Bill looked at her as if she were a child. "Mind control. If you did all the research I did, you would understand."

"When did you do all this 'research'? You never mentioned before about believing in this conspiracy."

"I did it after we found Marvin dead."

"That was yesterday. How much research could you have done?"

"I watched fifteen hours of videos. And I've just begun to scratch the surface. If you only knew what I know."

"If a dragon did it, why would the balcony door be locked from the inside?" Missy asked.

"It's a well-known fact Reptilians have telekinetic powers."

"Yeah, right."

"I'm sure it's on the internet somewhere," Bill said. "I'll find it and show you."

Agnes sighed. "If Marvin was murdered by a resident of our community, we need to find out and punish that vampire. Chasing after conspiracy theories doesn't help deliver justice."

"It's not a theory," Bill said. "It's the truth. The three of us are going to begin armed reconnaissance missions in the Everglades where Marvin shot that video."

"We are?" Sol asked.

"And we're going to recruit more members. The Reptilians picked the wrong vampires to mess with. We're going to end this invasion once and for all. Humans haven't been able to stop them. But we vampires, the masters of the night, will."

"You're nuts," Agnes said. "You do realize that, right?"

Bill tapped his pasty white forehead and smirked. "If you only knew what I know."

The three male vampires left the room, arguing about how much ammunition they should bring with them to the Everglades.

"This is quickly escalating out of control," Agnes said to Missy.

"I agree. I had hoped that there was a simple explanation for poor Marvin's sun-torching. It was just an innocent accident that he got locked out there, something faulty about the lock. But now it's turning into a circus. It couldn't get any more problematic."

"Good evening, ladies."

Missy jerked her head around to find Detective Fred Affird standing in the doorway of the card room. He was the nemesis of the vampires in Squid Tower, the werewolves in Seaweed Manor next door, and all supernatural creatures living in Jellyfish Beach. He had been on forced desk duty after recklessly discharging his firearm at a little old lady he believed to be a werewolf (she was). But apparently, he was back on active duty.

Missy had been wrong. Things *could* be more problematic.

"How can we help you, detective?" Agnes asked in a syrupy, sweet tone.

"Has there been a suspicious death of a resident here?"

"Why would you ask that?"

His lips tightened on his expressionless face. As usual, he wore sunglasses even at night and even when he was inside. He was tall, thin, and known to summarily execute supernaturals.

"I'm asking because I want to know."

"One of our dear residents recently passed away," Agnes said.

"Interesting," Affird said. "I did a database search and saw no record of a death. In fact, there aren't any records of deaths occurring here, ever."

"We're a healthy bunch of seniors," Agnes said.

"The residents who have passed away did so in the hospital or in hospice," Missy lied. Of course, Affird was correct. Everyone in Squid Tower was immortal.

"How did the deceased die?" the detective asked. "Natural causes or something suspicious?"

"Natural causes," Agnes and Missy said at the same time.

Affird's black eyebrows arched above his sunglass frames.

"And what was the cause?"

"Heart attack," Agnes said.

"Spontaneous combustion," Missy said.

Affird and Agnes looked at her with surprise. But Missy knew Squid Tower needed to explain why there was no corpse. They couldn't claim Marvin had been cremated, because Affird would check the records of the crematoriums.

"You've surely heard of spontaneous combustion," Missy said. "There have been several documented cases of people found burned to ashes with no external cause of the fire."

"In all my years on the force, I've never come across one," Affird said.

"You have now."

"Do you have any evidence of this?"

"The sun lounger he was found in has burn damage."

"Can I see it?"

Missy and Agnes exchanged worried glances.

"Yes," Agnes said. "Come with me."

The three rode the elevator to the fourth floor without talking. Affird allowed Missy to come, probably because he knew she was the community's home health nurse, and she was behaving like she knew exactly what happened.

Agnes unlocked the door to the condo with an extra set of keys Marvin had left with the management office. On this second visit to the unit, Missy noticed the desktop computer on the dining room table with a giant monitor and post-it notes affixed everywhere. A map of Florida was tacked to the wall with pushpins stuck in various locations. Paperback books about assorted conspiracy theories rose in stacks on the floor, on tables, on the kitchen counter.

Affird took it all in and wrote something on a notepad.

They went out onto the balcony. Agnes switched on the outside light.

"See?" Missy pointed to the sun lounger with the burned cushion.

Affird grunted.

"Marvin never smoked," Agnes said. "You can rule that out as a cause of the fire."

Missy wished she hadn't said that. The spontaneous combustion theory was already a stretch.

"Where are the remains?" Affird asked.

"Remains? There weren't any," Agnes said.

"The ashes."

"A wind gust from the northeast took them away," Missy said.

"Surely not all of them," Affird said.

"I believe one of his neighbors swept up a small amount into a freezer bag," Agnes said. "Mrs. Kinkuddy."

"Tell her I'm going to come by at a later date to get them for forensic testing."

Missy grew nervous. Was there a way a test could tell Marvin was a vampire? She hoped not.

"There were no other remains besides the ashes?" Affird asked.

"No," Agnes said.

"Hmm, the little I know about spontaneous human combustion—if it's even real—would suggest that the victim's feet or parts of his lower leg would have remained unburned."

"Nope. Marvin was one hundred percent consumed," Missy said.

"I see," Affird muttered as he scrawled more notes on his pad. Then he looked up at Agnes with a smug, knowing expression. "I'll be back to chat with you soon. I haven't visited your lovely community in a while. There are so many things I'd love to learn about the place. Who knows, when I can afford to stop working, maybe I'll retire here myself."

"You never said how you knew there was a death here," Agnes said.

"I'm a detective. I have sources everywhere."

On his way out, Affird did a once-over of the condo, probably looking for any signs of a struggle. Just as he was about to reach the front door to leave, he veered sharply into the kitchen. He yanked open the refrigerator. It was empty, except for bottled water and two pint bags labeled type O-positive whole blood.

Missy's stomach froze.

"Now, why would Mr. Nutley have blood in here?" Affird asked.

"He loves to donate it," Agnes said.

"A science experiment," Missy said over her at the same time.

"Which is it?" Affird asked. "Either answer sounds pretty far-fetched."

"To feed his pet vampire bat," Missy said. "Now, I remember. His beloved bat Fifi. She's already been adopted into a new forever home."

Affird chuckled. "Good one."

He opened the pantry and found it bare.

"Mr. Nutley didn't eat much," he said.

"We donated all his food to a food pantry," Agnes said.

"I see. How generous of you," Affird said, closing the pantry door. "Thank you for showing me around. I'll be in touch."

After he left, Missy and Agnes both let out huge sighs.

"Pet vampire bat?" Agnes asked.

"Well, it was more believable than him drawing pints of his own blood in his condo to donate."

"What matters is that awful detective is going to be a millstone around our necks again."

"How did he hear of Marvin's death?" Missy asked.

"That worries me. Is there an informer among us? I wish

22

he'd just leave us alone. But he's not going to stop poking around until he has proof we're vampires. How old do you think he is?"

"Late-forties, early fifties. Why?"

"We're a fifty-five-plus community," Agnes said. "Maybe I should take him up on his comment about retiring here."

"But wouldn't he need to be a vampire?"

Agnes gave an evil smile.

"That would save us all a bunch of trouble," Missy said.

3

DRAGONS KEEP GRUDGES

Oleg walked down the dirt road in the utter darkness of the moonless night. Being a vampire, he could see perfectly well, of course. Sol and Bill trudged ahead of him, weighed down by their body armor, semi-automatic rifles, pistols, grenades, and all the other gear Bill had hoarded as part of his hobby of pretending he was a one-man army.

Oleg had been in the military, while Bill and Sol hadn't. Bill behaved with the false bravado of a man who'd never put his life in danger on the battlefield. Oleg served over 230 years ago, leading a regiment of cavalry for Catherine the Great. Back then, honor and courage were what made a man, not how many weapons he collected. Tonight, Oleg carried only his old saber and a light rifle he borrowed from Bill.

He believed human weapons were unnecessary, given his lethal powers as a vampire, but he went along and armed himself, not knowing what beasts they might face.

Oleg was here tonight only out of curiosity. He didn't believe in the Reptilian conspiracy. He hadn't believed in dragons, either, though Marvin's video had been pretty convincing. Maybe the paranoid kook had used computer-generated imagery to create the dragon, though.

"Do you even know where you're leading us?" Sol asked Bill. Sol was a scrawny, bald fellow who looked like Nosferatu in a Boston Red Sox cap.

"Of course. We're very near where Marvin shot the Reptilian."

"How do you know? The Everglades is freaking enormous. And it all looks the same."

"I zoomed into the video and saw a sign in the background. Nine Mile Pond. That's where we're headed."

"You know, there's something that's been bugging me," Sol continued. "I did a little research, and Reptilians, when they're not in human form, look like, well, lizard people. Kind of like taller humans on two legs with lizard features. Not like dragons."

"Reptilians are shape-shifters," Bill said. "They can adopt any form they want."

"Then why would they become humans when they can become dragons? Dragons are cooler."

"Power. Don't you understand? They want to control the earth, and humans are the species that does. At least, for now."

"So, what are we supposed to do, just sit here and wait for a Reptilian to show up?" Sol asked.

"We're setting up an ambush point," Bill said.

Oleg, having been an actual military commander, was tired of his friends' cluelessness. He had come along to ease the monotony of his centuries-old existence. Anything to break up the boredom. But he'd had enough of passively following these clowns.

"Will you gentleman end this charade that you are human infantrymen?" Oleg said. "We are vampires, the deadliest predators on earth."

"Some say SEAL Team Six is the deadliest," Bill said.

"Enough!" Oleg shouted. The two other vampires snapped to attention. "Put away those infrared goggles, Bill. You're a vampire, for pity's sake! We will find the Reptilians using our vampire senses."

"You don't know how expensive these goggles were."

"Fan out and hunt," Oleg commanded. "Bill, continue down this road to the west. Sol, take that hiking trail toward the pond. I will follow this game trail to the south."

"Dividing our force in the face of the enemy?" Bill asked dubiously.

"We are vampires. I hunt alone."

As Oleg navigated a barely perceptible path made by animals through tall grasses, Sol's voice followed.

"Um, how do I know the difference between the scent of a reptile and a Reptilian?"

"A Reptilian will smell of human mixed with reptile," Bill said. "I thought that would be obvious."

Oleg pushed onward, eager to be away from the clowns. His super-sensitive olfactory sense detected various creatures in the area. There were alligators, of course, in a nearby creek. Several smaller reptile species were in abundance. Far in the distance, a Florida panther prowled. There were very few mammals around, thanks to the giant Burmese pythons in the area, some of which were nearby along the creek that held the gators. The pythons were an invasive species that had multiplied unchecked and eaten most of the mammals from deer to rodents.

Speaking of predators, a cloud of mosquitos hung around Oleg's head, like they would with any creature with blood, living or undead. They didn't bother vampires as much as they would humans, though.

Each time a mosquito went in for an attack, it would land, stick its proboscis into Oleg's skin and drink his blood. Yes, the irony of another creature drinking a vampire's blood. But vampire blood wasn't the same as a normal, living mammal's.

Soft popping sounds went off around Oleg's hands and neck. It was the sound of mosquitos exploding. One taste of the super-dense, hyper-potent blood of the larger bloodsucker made the tiny bloodsuckers' organs boil and detonate.

The best thing was their bites didn't even itch.

Oleg had hunted in the Everglades before, a century ago, before invasive pythons and invasive humans had knocked the environment off balance. After he'd been made into a vampire in his sixties, he remained in St. Petersburg, Russia, enjoying the lifestyle of his group of aristocratic vampires. But once the Russian Revolution reared its ugly head, he emigrated to America. There were plenty of humans to dine on in New York City, but his funds were tighter than they had been in the Old Country.

Then, he heard about the rampant land speculation going on in Florida. The thought of a new territory with little, if any, competition from other vampires was appealing. So, he hopped on a train and moved to Palm Beach and then Miami. He made a fortune selling residential swampland to unsuspecting buyers up north.

He couldn't deny knowing the lots were underwater because he went hunting in the area, feeding on the blood of small mammals to supplement his diet. He knew what he was doing, but the buyers he'd defrauded were just stupid humans, so he felt no guilt. Plus, everyone else in real estate down here was involved in dubious schemes. The appetite to buy in Florida while the market was hot was so strong it overcame common sense back in those days.

The victims of a predator made it so easy, sometimes. That wasn't the case here in the Everglades.

He'd caught the scent of recent death, and now he found it. Floating in the still, dark water of a winding creek was the strangest sight Oleg ever saw around here. A giant python, close to twenty feet long, lay against the bank, dead. It was grossly misshaped, its middle section taking on the contours of the meal it had swallowed.

A buck, one that was clearly too large for the hungry snake. The deer had also put up a fight. Both antlers had broken through the stomach and skin of the python, killing the gluttonous predator.

Humans aren't the only stupid creatures in Florida, Oleg mused.

As if to mock his arrogance, giant jaws clamped down on his right ankle from behind.

It was a gator, hoping to dine on a vampire. It was a big one, over ten feet long.

The gator yanked on Oleg's ankle to drag him into the water. There, it would get him into a tighter hold, pulling him underwater and performing death rolls until Oleg drowned.

Oleg would not allow that to happen. His supernatural strength helped him stand his ground as the gator tried to pull him to the water. But as strong as he was, he could not open the reptile's jaws. No creature on earth was strong enough to do that. Oleg could shoot the creature, but that was too easy. It was what Bill would do. He could also drive the point of his cavalry saber between the gator's eyes and kill it. But that, too, was beneath him, even though the pain in his ankle was growing agonizing.

Instead, Oleg gazed into the gator's eyes and waved his hand slowly. Yes, even a lizard brain could be mesmerized by an experienced vampire. Oleg concentrated on a vision of the gator releasing its jaws.

A few seconds later, the gator did exactly that.

"Thank you, my friend," Oleg said. "I wish you better hunting."

The Everglades was a microcosm of the world at large: fragile beauty mixed with pitiless savagery. It made him feel like a superior creature again to have shown the alligator mercy.

He questioned the superiority of vampires only a few minutes later when shots rang out in the distance. So many shots it sounded like successive volleys by two armies lined up against one another on the battlefield.

Then a hand grenade exploded.

Oleg needed to reach the morons before the U.S. Park Service did.

BILL AND SOL hadn't gone their separate ways, as Oleg had ordered. But it turned out they had the right formula to find a Reptilian.

They were about a half mile further along the road the three vampires had begun on. Bill was prone on the dirt, aiming his assault rifle into a thick growth of small trees. Sol was crouched in the undergrowth, aiming in the same direction.

"Cease this undisciplined firing," Oleg said as he jogged up to them. "You'll alert every human within miles."

"We got one!" Bill said excitedly. "We got him with several rounds. Except my dunderhead friend didn't take a video of it like I asked him to."

"It happened so quickly," Sol said. "I was busy shooting."

"Where is it?" Oleg asked.

"The Reptilian? Um, it disappeared."

"You mean it escaped?"

"When it showed up, it sort of materialized out of shimmering air," Bill explained. "Sol and I engaged it, hitting it multiple times. It was on the ground. But it crawled backwards, wounded, and disappeared into the shimmering air again."

"Shimmering air?"

"Yeah. In that clearing over there. The air was shimmering like water."

"It isn't now," Oleg said.

"Well, it was before. I was looking at the clearing, and suddenly the air began shimmering in a big circle. The Reptilian walked out of it. After the Reptilian went back in, the shimmering disappeared. The shimmering took the Reptilian with it."

"Shimmering."

"It's true," Sol said. "It happened just like Bill said. Only it wasn't a Reptilian we shot. It was a dragon. A dragon just like the ones in storybooks and movies."

"It was a Reptilian," Bill insisted. "It was returning to earth in order to transform into a human and run the U.S. government."

"It was a dragon," Sol said.

"You saw Marvin's video. It clearly showed a human turning into a reptile," Bill said.

"There are lots of types of reptiles. This one was the flying, fire-breathing type. Not a seven-foot-tall, bipedal, human-lizard hybrid."

"Look, if it can transform from human to dragon, it can change into any darned type of reptile it wants," Bill said petulantly.

"There might be repercussions if you guys killed a dragon," Oleg said. "Frankly, I didn't know dragons exist, but since they do, we need to make sure they don't seek vengeance."

"Oh, they'll think twice before messing with us," Bill said. "The purpose of tonight's mission was to send a message that planet Earth is not going to take their crap anymore. We know what they're doing, and we're going to stop them. Even if we have to do it by killing one Reptilian at a time."

"One dragon at a time," Sol said.

"Enough already. Tomayto-tomahto. Reptilian-dragon. Whatever."

"Get your gear together and collect any used cartridges you can find," Oleg said. "We should get out of here. I have an uneasy feeling."

"What do you mean? With all this firepower, we're unstoppable."

When they finally returned to where they had parked the SUV, they discovered that, actually, they *were* stoppable.

The SUV was a burned husk on the side of the road. The crumpled, charred remains smoldered on the singed grass.

"They didn't stop us," Bill said. "They merely delayed us."

"Right. Try getting a taxi or a ride-hail to come out here in the middle of the Everglades," Oleg said. "We'd better get walking before the sun comes up."

MISSY HAD JUST GONE to sleep when the voice appeared in her head.

Missy, we need to talk. It was a voice she fondly remembered, the slight drawl of her dragon friend, Ronnie.

Ronnie! I'm so glad to hear from you, she thought soundlessly. *I saw a video of a dragon being shot. Was that you? Are you okay?"*

Yes, it was me. And yes, I'm okay. Thanks to my scale armor and our healer, my wounds were minor. But I'm freaking mad.

The video showed you shifting from human to dragon. When did you get that ability?

When I fully matured to adulthood. I inherited special powers that most dragons don't have. It's why I was destined to become their king.

And it's why the vampire who shot you believed you were a Reptilian from outer space, she said.

That's crazy.

Missy agreed. She wanted to ask him if he incinerated Marvin without sounding like she was accusing him.

The vampire who shot you is dead, she said.

And one of our dragons is dead, shot multiple times by foolish vampires in the Everglades. She had just passed through a gateway from the In Between when they shot her. She managed to crawl back through the gateway before it disappeared, but we couldn't save her, even with magic.

I'm so sorry, she said.

Humanoids and dragons have not fought for many centuries, his voice said. Mostly because dragons were almost wiped out. We left the populated areas of Europe and Asia to find places where we could live in peace and reproduce. Often, we must take refuge in the In Between. It was working out for us. But now your vampires have ruined it.

I apologize for the vampires who killed your friend. They're misguided old guys, crazy with conspiracy theories. I'll tell their leader they should be punished.

It's too late, Ronnie said sadly. *The dragons, especially the older lords, want war.*

Oh, my.

War against humans, vampires, and all humanoids.

That seems excessive, don't you think?

Dragons keep grudges, Ronnie said. *Centuries of being slain by human warriors and knights looking for publicity. We've held grudges ever since.*

There must be a way to avoid war, Missy said.

I am the king of the dragons, and if I refuse what they want, I will be dethroned by the dragon lords. Some of them are hundreds of years old, and I'm just a baby in comparison. They've reluctantly accepted my rule because of the prophecy. And now, they insist upon war. It is beyond my control now.

Oh, my.

I will do my best to keep it as a limited war. I will try to make sure innocents like you aren't harmed. But if your hot-headed vampires do anything reckless, the hostilities will escalate. Please give this warning to your vampire friends.

I will. I'm so sorry for your loss.

I am sorry, in advance, for those you will lose.

Her mind went silent. Ronnie's consciousness had left it.

She reached for her phone on the bedside table and texted Agnes.

"Reign in Bill and his gun-buddies. They killed a dragon, and now the dragons are going to war."

4

HOW ARE YOUR KIDNEYS?

Family dramas can pop up at any time, usually inconvenient ones. Here the earth was, at the precipice of a cataclysmic war between dragons and humans, and Missy's mother called.

The mother who gave her up as an infant. The black-magic sorceress who tried to kill her on at least two occasions. The woman who shouldn't even have the chutzpah to call herself a mother.

And now she was on the phone. Missy took the call in the lobby of Squid Tower, in between two patient appointments.

"Hello, dear," her mother said with nauseating sweetness.

"Ruth? What could you possibly want?"

Ophelia Lawthorne was her biological mother's real name, but she changed it to Ruth Bent to avoid bill collectors and the enforcers from the Magic Guild.

"To say hello. See how you're doing. You can call me by my real name, dear. We're family."

"To see how I'm doing? I'm alive and breathing, no thanks to you. *Ophelia*. Last time we saw each other, you paralyzed me with a spell and was about to launch me through a fifth-story window."

"Oh, the things I do sometimes." Her mother laughed nervously. "That was business, dear. You were interfering with my spell to kill all the manatees in Florida for a client. I was contractually obligated to perform that spell."

"You could have put me out with a sleep spell," Missy said. "You didn't have to attempt to kill me."

"You know me. I'm all business."

"All psychopath is more like it."

"I regret that I'm not always good at showing affection."

"That has to be the biggest understatement in all of history. Your lack of affection began when you gave me up as a baby."

"I explained to you why I had to do that. Your father had just died. The Magic Guild had banished me from San Marcos and recommended I give you up."

Missy didn't believe the Magic Guild had anything to do with Ophelia giving her up for adoption. But the truth was, she had a much better childhood than she would have if she had lived with the sorceress-for-hire. She was taken in by her father's cousin and lived a normal life in a loving home, although a home where magic was not welcome. For good reason. When the magick in Missy's genes became active, she repressed it.

She was a late bloomer as a witch, not having put effort into it until she was nearing midlife. After burning out from the stress and emotional toil of being a nurse in the intensive care unit, and having her husband leave her for a man who was a vampire. And after her ex-husband, after being turned, was staked to death by a rogue cop. That was when Missy took the job as a home health nurse for an agency that catered to vampires, werewolves, and other supernaturals who couldn't go to human doctors.

And that was when she turned inward and discovered powers she didn't know she had. She cultivated them and learned earth magick, a benign form that used the energies of the elements in its spells. Unlike the black magic of her biological mother, which leveraged the powers of demons, death, and Hell.

So, yes, she was better off not being raised by Ophelia.

"You've been well, then?" Ophelia asked.

"Yes. And you?" Missy asked, to be polite.

"Oh, I've been better. I'm getting quite on in years, you know."

"Yes." Missy knew Ophelia also chain-smoked and had an unhealthy diet.

"And how are your kidneys?" Ophelia asked.

"I beg your pardon?"

"Your kidneys. How are they doing?"

"They're fine." Missy, who went to a human doctor, knew this to be a fact. "Why do you ask?"

The answer to her question sank in before her mother answered.

"Do you think you could spare a kidney? You only need one, you know. You'll never know the other one's gone. Because I could sure use one. Assuming we're a match."

"You have kidney failure?"

"Yep. I've been doing dialysis three times a week, and my doctor says I need a transplant."

Missy realized she'd been holding her breath for an unhealthy interval.

"Can't you heal your kidneys with magic?" she asked.

"Nope. I practice black magic. I put hexes on fields to kill crops. I make people grow hideous warts while their hair falls out. I summon demons to kill the innocent. Healing magic, it's not."

"Don't you also raise the dead? Isn't that sort of a healing process?"

"Nope. Totally different principle. Plus, my kidneys aren't technically dead. And if they were, who would want zombie kidneys?"

"I see," Missy said.

What was the best way to politely decline the request for a kidney?

"You know, I've been awfully busy lately. I just don't have time to undergo major surgery."

"You call giving enemas to constipated vampires busy? That's more important than saving a life?"

"Asks the woman who tried to kill me. And not just at the office building. There was the time before that when you tried with a giant mosquito and an enthralled ogre."

"Missy, you need to learn to forgive and forget. It's unhealthy to carry resentments inside you."

Missy didn't add that she suspected her mother was responsible for her father's death. She'd learned her father was also a witch, as he called himself. Others referred to him as a wizard. Either way, he was exceptionally wise and powerful, using white magick as Missy did, never dabbling in black magic like his wife.

One night, he was killed in their kitchen in what was officially called a freak dishwasher accident. Most in the magic community believed a demon was at fault.

Missy believed the demon was summoned by her mother, who was jealous for being overshadowed by her husband's magic. Her mother, of course, denied it.

Missy had resolved to find the truth someday.

"Oh, it's my fault for feeling resentment?" Missy asked. "And how do I know this isn't a scheme to get me onto an operating room table, under anesthesia, where you can kill me?

"I'm your mother, the one who gave you life."

"You wouldn't even be talking to me now if you didn't need something from me."

"I need life. You can give me life."

Well, when she puts it that way, it's even harder to say no.

"Aren't you on an organ donor registry?"

"Of course. But the wait could be longer than the time I have left."

"Oh."

"Can you, at least, find out if we're a match? That's all I ask right now. See if we're a match, and then you can decide what to do."

"Okay. I'll let you know."

Missy didn't need another weight on her mind.

Especially not as screams came from outside, followed by the dull *thump* of an explosion. Squid Tower's fire alarm went off.

AS MARVIN PROVED, fire is one of the few ways a vampire's eternal existence could be terminated. Consequently, vampires are terrified of fire. The lovely fireplace in the first-floor community room had never been, and will never be, used.

Squid Tower was equipped with a smoke-triggered sprinkler system, so the fire was most likely extinguished in whichever unit set off the alarm. But that didn't stop nearly the entire population of the building from scurrying downstairs and flooding from the exits into the parking lot and meticulously groomed grounds.

Word quickly spread that the fire had been in only one condo, and it had not been caused by something mundane such as lint in a dryer duct.

Since it was night when everyone was up, more than one resident reported seeing a giant flying creature approach the building from the ocean, hover opposite the fourth floor, and belch a stream of fire into the balcony of Bill Meany. Bill was not on his balcony. He was in his den watching a commando movie, but the flames melted the sliding glass door to the balcony, which exploded, and then the fire poured into his living room, turning his couch into charcoal.

"See, it's the same thing that happened to Marvin," an obviously unscathed Bill said to anyone who would listen. "The Reptilians know we're on to them and want to silence us."

If a dragon had killed Marvin, why were the burns so surgically exact? Missy wondered. Bill's balcony next door, though, had been completely charred. Perhaps, the difference in the flames' radius was intentional on the dragon's part. Missy wasn't so sure.

"We need to kick some Reptilian butt before they burn down all of Squid Tower!" Bill called to the crowd milling by the shuffleboard courts

The Jellyfish Beach Fire Department had arrived, and the

residents stood as far away as possible, worried about how pale and lifeless their faces would look in the strobe lights of the fire engines.

"Who will take up arms and join Sol, Oleg, and me in fighting the invaders?"

The crowd now was trying to stay as far away from Bill as possible, flowing into the pickleball courts.

"Wait one minute," Agnes said sternly. She strode toward Bill, surprisingly formidable on her little legs and quad-cane. Henrietta, her top aide, followed in her mobility scooter. Something about vampires in mobility scooters truly frightened Missy.

Behind Henrietta walked Maria, an inexperienced vampire in her twenties, whom Agnes had taken in. The young woman had been adrift and homeless until Agnes stepped in as a grandmotherly figure. Maria had also wanted to kill Missy, which made for awkward social moments like this.

"You will *not* escalate things with the dragons," Agnes warned Bill.

"Reptilians."

"Call them whatever you want, but they are dragons, a species with a long history of enmity with humanoids. Their king is being pushed by his council to engage in total war against us and humans. He is trying to talk them into peace. We do *not* need you to make matters worse."

"They tried to kill me tonight," Bill said. "They could have burned down the entire building."

"But they didn't," Agnes said.

"You killed a dragon last night," Missy said. "You started this."

"The dragon who killed Marvin started it."

"Marvin shot him with no provocation."

"Stop the hostilities or you will be punished by the Board," Agnes said.

Henrietta drove her scooter right up to Bill, almost running over his toes.

"I'm not going to be intimidated by your thug," Bill said.

The folks in any retirement community can be cranky and quarrelsome at times. In one populated by vampires, bad tempers were even more common. Being trapped in a seventy-year-old body for hundreds of years could turn anyone mean.

Schwartz wandered onto the pickleball courts wearing tennis shorts and carrying a racquet bag.

"Hey, I got a match scheduled in five minutes. Everyone, get off the court."

"You don't care that our building almost burned down?" Bill asked.

"I do care, and I blame you. You and your moron militia."

"Easy for you to say, since you depend on brave men like us to defend you."

"Ha! What a joke! I heard you're the reason the dragon came here and torched your place."

"They killed Marvin."

"It would be very convenient for us to believe that, wouldn't it?" Schwartz taunted.

"What are you trying to say?"

"Everyone knows you and Marvin didn't get along."

"Are you implying I killed him?" Bill asked with exaggerated outrage.

"It was easy for you to see when he was on the balcony. Then, all you had to do was sneak into his condo and lock the sliding glass door."

"Why are you taking the side of the dragons instead of your fellow vampires? I'm not talking to you anymore, dragon lover," Bill said, walking away.

"Can the rest of you follow him off the pickleball courts, please?" Schwartz asked.

Agnes sighed. "We don't need a war with the dragons when we have one amongst ourselves."

"That's what the dragons want," Bill said as he walked past her.

"If we all need to fight the dragons, the only one who could unite and inspire us would be you, Agnes," Henrietta said.

"If that is true, then I'm the one who must prevent us from having to fight at all."

5

THE PARLEY

"You've got to be kidding me," Matt said, after he nearly choked on his coffee. "You're going to parley with dragons?"

"I shouldn't have said anything," Missy murmured.

She looked around the outdoor cafe where they were having breakfast to make sure no one was eavesdropping. The place faced the beach and was where they met most often with their opposing night-day working hours.

"Let's get real," Matt said. "I met Ronnie when you were nursing him to health. I know about dragons. And I've kept my knowledge secret ever since, just as I promised I would."

"I know, but—"

"We have a sacred agreement between us," Matt said.

"It's not exactly sacred. It's—"

"Sacred to me. I've agreed to help you investigate things. I do the shoe-leather reporting, the cold calls, the digging through archives, all the hard, tedious, thankless work. And I do it without getting stories out of it that would help my career. Because I care about you."

"And because I introduce you to aspects of the supernatural world that you would have no access to without me."

"Right. It's a quid pro quo. And a very effective one, I should say."

"Yes. I guess so."

"So, I want to go with you to this parley," Matt said.

"Why?"

"It's a historic moment. Humans, vampires, and dragons reaching a peace agreement."

"Technically, it's just between dragons and vampires," Missy said. "Humans aren't part of the war, yet. The only reason I'm there is I'm the go-between, since I'm friends with Ronnie."

"You said the dragons had declared war on all humanoids. It's only a matter of time before mortal humans get caught up in it. And personally, I don't believe any dragon is a match for an F-18 Hornet fighter jet."

"I'm not sure I agree, but let's hope it doesn't come to that."

"I should go with you as a bodyguard."

She smiled as she looked at his slim physique. He was in good shape, but not at all shaped like a bodyguard.

"You can't write a story about the meeting. Or take pictures or video."

"I know, I know. I promise."

"Okay," she said before taking a last bite of her crepes.

"When is it?"

"Tonight. On the roof of the Jellyfish Beach Hotel. Meet me on the sidewalk out front at quarter to midnight."

The hotel was chosen as neutral ground. Agnes didn't feel comfortable meeting in the Everglades, and Ronnie felt the same about Squid Tower. The hotel was the tallest building in town, not counting the other condo towers the humanoids wouldn't have access to. In a rooftop meeting, the dragons could fly in and out with ease and less chance of an ambush. The humanoids could escape to the stairwell, if necessary. It seemed to be the best choice for both parties.

The door to the roof, at the top of the stairwell, was not locked in case guests had to be evacuated from the roof in a fire. Missy used her magick to disable the security cameras. So, she, Agnes, and Matt stood on the roof and waited, enjoying the moonlit view of the Atlantic Ocean in front of them and the glow of lights of Jellyfish Beach stretching to the west.

Missy worried that the dragons flying in would be picked up on radar, until she figured they would probably come through a nearby gateway from the In Between.

She was correct. Not far offshore, the air shimmered. And two dragons appeared, flying over the beach, and landing gracefully on the hotel roof. It was Ronnie and a brown dragon she didn't recognize.

"Thank you for coming," Agnes said.

"Thank you, as well," said Ronnie aloud, not telepathically.

Ronnie introduced the other dragon as Godwin, a more dragon-like name than Ronnie, in Missy's opinion. She introduced Matt. And then they got down to business.

"I have no interest in war," Ronnie said. "The lords on my council are clamoring for it, though. They conveniently forget all the suffering of both our species when dragons and humanoids fought each other."

"The vampires who attacked your dragons do not represent my vampires," Agnes said. "We are elderly and peaceful. We wish to spend eternity enjoying friendships and Bingo night.

The males who attacked you are deluded old fools who have been brainwashed by conspiracy theories."

"I thought as much," Ronnie said. "Though, I've seen enough humans to know they're a violent species. I know less about vampires, but it seems they have the same minds as humans."

"And some of them have very small minds," Missy said.

"We are proposing you give us one of them."

"One what?" Agnes asked.

"One of the vampires who killed our dragon," Ronnie replied. "I will graciously forgive the wounds I experienced. But Dragon law follows the principle of an eye for an eye, a tooth for a tooth, a tail for a tail. Our tails don't regrow like other lizards, by the way."

Missy knew she shouldn't be surprised about the demand, but she was. Agnes would never agree to it. Just like Ronnie's dragons were demanding blood or else they would overthrow him, Agnes would be thrown out of her position as HOA president and community leader if she sacrificed one of her own.

"Though your offer is tempting when it comes to a certain vampire, I cannot accept," Agnes said. "Vampire justice doesn't work that way."

"Don't you punish murderers?"

"Yes, but we punish them ourselves. We don't hand them over to another party."

"My dragons will not be satisfied until they see a guilty vampire killed. Those who watched through the gateway to the Everglades said one of the two vampires who attacked was deadlier. He wore a black beret."

Bill, Missy thought. No surprise.

Agnes was silent while she considered her options. The truth was, Bill should be tried for murder. Or something. It's kind of tricky punishing a deadly creature for killing things. Vampires kill humans all the time, though it's strongly discouraged. And a vampire who does so too close to home can be punished severely because it endangers the entire vampire community.

The same should apply to dragons. They're not mere animals one can hunt in the wild. And if killing a dragon endangers the vampire community, then Bill and Sol should be punished, banned from the community or, even, staked.

Missy knew that banning them would not satisfy the dragons.

"We will put them on trial," Agnes said. "If they are sentenced to be staked, you will be given proof of their executions."

"If they are sentenced?" Godwin asked angrily. "*If?*"

A loud bang came from behind them as the door to the stairs opened. Missy turned to see Bill leaping out, dressed in black tactical gear and weighed down by too many weapons to count.

"Why are you talking to these evil Reptilians?" he asked Agnes. "They'll fool you with mind control."

"How did you know we were here?" Agnes asked.

"I followed you." He tapped his head beneath his black beret. "I'm cleverer than you believe."

He aimed a semi-automatic rifle, held at his hip like an action-movie character, toward the dragons.

"Go back to wherever you came from," he said. "Go to the fires of Hell."

The dragons were already in the air when the first rounds sprayed from the weapon, missing them.

"No!" Matt shouted as he dove and tackled Bill to the ground as more rounds went off.

Hovering twenty feet in the air, Godwin sent a torrent of fire toward the two men. They were partly protected by the roof of the stairwell, so Missy couldn't tell if they'd been hurt.

The dragons streaked across the sky toward a shimmering spot near where they had first appeared.

Matt and Bill groaned and grunted as they wrestled. A loud bang was followed by the hiss of a projectile streaking from beneath them, narrowly missing Agnes and Missy as it headed toward the gateway.

The dragons disappeared. Then an explosion lit up the sky.

"What in God's name are you doing with a rocket-propelled grenade?" Matt cried.

Light applause arose from the beach below. It was hotel guests who believed a fireworks display had begun.

"You idiot!" Agnes shouted at Bill. "Do you realize what you have done?"

"I've struck a blow for freedom," Bill said, squeezing out from beneath Matt.

Before Missy could cast a spell to immobilize the militant vampire, he disappeared down the stairwell.

Matt groaned and tried unsuccessfully to stand. Tendrils of smoke arose from the back of his pants and shirt.

"I've been burned," he said.

"We've all been burned," Agnes muttered under her breath.

MISSY WENT with Matt to the hospital. He had first-degree and small patches of second-degree burns. Ironically, tackling Bill shielded the vampire from the fire. Bill appeared to be fine when he sprinted down the stairs.

Matt was lucky the roof of the stairwell had blocked the full blast of the dragon breath, and that it was a short blast. Dragons could melt steel with their fire.

In addition to his burns, the backs of Matt's clothes were mostly burned away. The entire seat of his pants was missing. Despite his bright-red burns, his naked butt was pretty cute, Missy thought.

Agnes texted the news that Bill had not returned to his condo, which was still habitable despite the earlier fire damage. She didn't expect him to return any time soon. Even with a brain turned to mush by conspiracy theories, he knew he was likely to face punishment by his community.

Missy was shocked by Bill's going off the deep end. He'd always been a kook, but a harmless one. He'd been very helpful to Agnes and Missy in previous adventures. But now, he was a lost cause.

And it seemed peace was a lost cause, too. Missy dreaded what would come after Bill violated the sanctity of the parley by attacking the dragons. They had been humiliated and narrowly escaped with their lives.

They would surely retaliate. But she didn't know how to deescalate the situation. The dragons would never trust her again to negotiate. A whacked-out extremist named Bill ruined it for everyone.

Her phone rang. It was her mother again.

"Yes," Missy said, making no effort to warm her icy tone.

"Have you been tested yet?"

"Only my patience has been tested. What are you talking about?"

"To see if you'll be a compatible kidney donor," her mother said crossly. "I went over this already. The more compatible we are, the fewer anti-rejection drugs I'll have to take and the less magic I'll need to use afterwards."

"To be completely honest, I haven't decided yet if I want to donate. Things have been hectic here. We're on the verge of a cataclysmic war that could end the world."

"Maybe if you weren't so wrapped up in your little life, you'd feel some concern for your mother who has end-stage kidney disease. I could die if I don't get a donation. Isn't that more important than the world ending? I've had other donors lined up, but they didn't work out. As a blood relative, you have the best chance of being compatible."

"Right," Missy said, not fully listening.

The television mounted on the wall of Matt's room showed a news video of a house on fire. Was this the result of a dragon attack? She hoped it wasn't.

She waited for several agonizing moments for the scrolling chyron at the bottom of the screen to reveal the cause: a meth lab explosion.

"Unless it was spontaneous human combustion," Missy muttered.

"What are you saying?" her mother asked. "I could die without your help."

"So, what does this testing entail?"

"Don't you know? You were a nurse."

"I was in the ICU. I didn't work with organ transplantation."

"They need to know your blood type."

That was easy. Missy was AB-positive. Her vampire patients swore AB was the tastiest blood type. Which didn't make her feel happy at all.

"And they need to do tissue sampling. Some sort of anti . . . anti . . ."

"Antigens?"

"Yes. And maybe test your urine and run some dye through you. And some other stuff."

Was that too much work to save her mother's life? When you considered how evil the woman was, it just might be.

"As my own flesh and blood, you're my best hope," her mother said. "You can't turn your back on me in the darkest moment of my life."

Missy was certain her mother had experienced darker moments, most of which were of her making and affected someone else.

"I'll see if I can find time for the testing. I'll let you know. Bye." Missy clicked off.

She had a calling to help others. It was the reason she went into nursing in the first place and transitioned into home health. If she could find compassion for supernatural monsters, she could find it for just about anyone.

For her black-hearted mother, too? That was a trickier question.

Not only had her mother tried to kill her, but she might also have the blood of Missy's father on her hands. Could she really give this woman one of her precious kidneys?

Last time she had a near-fatal entanglement with her mother, Missy had vowed to find out who was responsible for her father's death. If he had died from human hands, she wanted to know whose. If a demon did, in fact, kill him, then who summoned the demon?

And if her mother was guilty, she could get her darn kidney from someone else.

There was nothing to do but wait until the dragons retaliated. It was the perfect time to leave town.

She announced this to Matt.

"You're going where?" He asked, lying on his stomach in his hospital bed. He would be released tomorrow.

"San Marcos."

"Why?"

"Long story."

6

FREAK DISHWASHER ACCIDENT

The *San Marcos Record* had digitalized its stories from the period when Missy's father died. When Missy first learned she was adopted, and that her birth parents had died, she had found the brief article reporting the tragedy and kept a copy.

"Theodore Lawthorne was declared dead at his home after the family's brand-new dishwasher, in the middle of its rinse cycle, had sprung open, jettisoning its contents, and impaling the victim with salad tongs," the news story read. "The whereabouts of his spouse, Ophelia Lawthorne, are unknown. The couple's infant daughter was found sleeping in a bedroom by first responders. At press time, the appliance manufacturer has not replied to requests for comment, but no similar fatality caused by a residential dishwasher has ever been recorded."

That this was an accident was highly suspect. But the police had believed it, and so had the medical examiner.

Afterwards, everyone thought her mother had died, too,

from some mysterious cause. Missy didn't find out she was still alive, and living in rural Central Florida, until recently.

Decades later, Missy heard from Arch Mage Bob, the head of the San Marcos Magic Guild, informing her the incident involved a demon, and her mother may have been the summoner.

Jellyfish Beach didn't have a magic guild, nor did most other places in Florida. It was only in the oldest cities, with the deepest traditions of other-worldly activity, that supernatural guilds held sway. The guilds regulated their members' activities as well as provided safety. And the guilds ensured that humans never found out that witches, wizards, werewolves, and vampires lived in their midst.

There were so few witches in Jellyfish Beach and surrounding Crab County that there was no need for a guild and the requirement to pay dues to it. But Missy believed the area's vampires would behave much better if they belonged to a guild of their own.

To investigate her father's death, Missy would need to work with the Magic Guild in San Marcos. She wasn't looking forward to dealing with Arch Mage Bob again. They'd butted heads in the past, to put it mildly. But she didn't have any choice. He seemed to have forgiven Ronnie, the dragon, for dropping him into a cesspool at the local sewage treatment plant.

Matt was back home, recovering nicely from his burns. He agreed to cat-sit Missy's two gray tabbies, visiting them at least twice a day while she was gone.

Before she left, she gave him a quick peck on the cheek. She hadn't planned on doing so; she wasn't a kissy-huggy kind of person. It just seemed right to show him a little affection.

Preventing him from hoping they could be more than friends wasn't so critical now.

She was a mile down the road before the tingle on her lips wore off.

The five-hour drive to San Marcos was not kind to her ancient Toyota. It took two magick spells and a quart of oil to keep her trusty mare galloping at a steady pace up I-95. Missy was a more conservative driver in her midlife, but she still had the urge to speed now and then. Her car wouldn't allow it, though. She remained in the right lane with the RVs and the old folks driving cars almost as old as they were.

Once she made it to San Marcos, came the difficult part. Who from the Magic Guild would be willing to help her? Magician protocol dictated that she begin by going through official channels.

Which meant Arch Mage Bob. And Bob never answered phone calls or texts. So, she had to drive to the surf shop he owned by the beach.

It was a giant store, with sunglasses and flip-flops for tourists in the front, clothing and swimsuits in the middle, and surfboards in the rear.

She asked a clerk if Bob was in. He wasn't. She went to the very back of the store where the workshop-office was. It was for employees only, but she walked inside anyway.

The air smelled of resin and cigars. A board being shaped by hand lay atop sawhorses.

"You again?"

"Hello, Florence," Missy said to the bird on a wooden perch-stand by the desk. She was an African Grey parrot with magical talent and human intelligence. "Do you know where Bob is?"

"He's surfing up by the pier," the bird said, punctuated by a squawk. "What do you want?"

"I'm investigating something from long, long ago. My father's death."

"Ah, I remember that."

Missy was shocked. "You do?"

"Hey, I wasn't born yesterday. I'm eighty-seven. I remember when he was murdered."

"You look great for your—wait. You said 'murdered?'"

"I did. We all knew it wasn't an accident."

"A demon did it?" Missy asked.

"That's what I believe. A high-ranking demon, they say. At the level where only a top black-magic sorcerer could summon it."

"Was the summoner my mother?"

The parrot gave a low whistle that ascended to a high note. "No one knows."

"Did the Guild do a full investigation?"

"I'm sure they did, although they never ruled it was a death-by-demon," said Florence.

"Well, that's why I'm here. I want to settle this question."

"It happened a long time ago. And black magic sorcerers are good at covering up their tracks. That's why no one knows the truth."

"Or maybe someone knows the truth, and they're not talking."

The parrot squawked, and Missy said goodbye. She drove up Highway A1A toward the pier, because she needed Bob's permission and guidance to get started.

She found the Arch Mage a mile south of the pier. Missy didn't know much about surfing, but the day must have offered good conditions, because many surfers were out. They clustered at various places up and down the beach. Bob was easy to spot, carving a big wave in his shaggy blond hair and middle-aged beer gut. A half dozen younger surfers were near him, all wearing wet suits because of the cool weather. Bob was the only person not wearing one. He probably intended to look macho, but Missy was certain he was using magic to stay warm.

After standing on the beach while he rode the next wave, she finally caught his eye and waved to him. When he reached the shore, he carried his board out. Missy walked to the edge of the surf to greet him.

"Thank you for sending me a copy of your grimoire," he said, smiling with impossibly white teeth. "The wizard knew some very interesting spells. Now, what brings you up to San Marcos?"

She explained her mission.

"Ah, that won't be easy. I was too young back then to be part of the investigation, you know, but I remember it was controversial."

"It was?"

"Yeah, there was, like, some corruption in the Guild back then. Some say your mother wasn't the only one messing around with black magic. You should speak with Wendall. He'd know more than me about those days."

"I hoped to speak with him, but I needed your permission to poke around on your turf."

Bob laughed. "You can poke around all you want, but I can't promise you the results you want."

"Understood. So where can I find Wendall? Can I have his number or email?"

"He doesn't have either. He's as off the grid as you can be

without living in remote wilderness. You'll have to find him wherever he's fishing. I'd try looking for him at the pier today."

"I will. Thank you."

"Keep me updated if you learn anything new," Bob said as she turned to go.

While she walked to the beach parking lot, she wondered how she could find anything the original investigation by the Guild hadn't found.

She reached her car in the sandy lot. An SUV was idling behind it, waiting for another spot to become available. She got the attention of the two men inside and signaled she was going to back out of her spot.

She unlocked her car, opened the door, and a beefy hand on a muscular arm grabbed the edge.

"You need to come with us," the man said close to her ear.

He put an arm around her and practically carried her back the way she had come to the waiting SUV. A second man stood by the open rear door. He searched her pockets and took her phone.

Missy filled her lungs before she screamed, but the first man pushed a folded beach towel into her face, muffling her. The two men lifted her and pushed her into the SUV's backseat. The first man slid into the seat next to her. Soon afterward, the other guy jumped into the driver's seat. Their SUV rolled slowly out of the lot in no particular hurry.

She began reciting a sleep spell to disable the men, but the one beside her pushed the towel so hard into her mouth, she tasted blood. Soon, the SUV was speeding down the road, so she didn't try again and risk putting the driver to sleep.

She wracked her brain for another spell to use. The problem was, her magick was benevolent. She didn't have an arsenal of offensive spells to take down enemies. She wasn't that kind of witch.

There was a protection spell she often used for defensive purposes. Now that she was already a captive, it wasn't much help. And the big guy was sitting right up against her. He'd probably end up inside the protection bubble with her.

What else was there?

She knew a good itching spell. It came in handy for distracting aggressive dogs, but she didn't see the utility in this situation. There was also the tickling spell. It would disable the guy guarding her, but she couldn't use it on the driver, or he would crash. And she couldn't jump out of the vehicle at this speed.

Maybe it would be best to try something at their destination.

"You were as easy to find as the lady said you would be," said the man guarding her.

Missy had a bad feeling about who this "lady" might be.

They were on the road a long time. After exiting the interstate, they headed west and south, on state and county roads, past farms and forests, warehouses, and Baptist churches. She saw a town name she recognized on a water tower and realized what part of Central Florida this was.

It was near where her mother lived.

WHEN THE SUV pulled into the dirt parking lot of an abandoned orange-packing facility, Missy was surprised. She had expected to be taken to her mother's dingy old house in the woods, not this barn-like structure in the middle of orange groves.

She had remained quiet, even after they'd removed the towel from her mouth. Not anymore.

"Where are we, and why did you bring me here?"

"You're in bumble-puck, Florida, and you're here because we were paid to bring you here," said the big guy who had ridden beside her. "And this is where we will part ways."

The driver got out, opened the door on her left, and pulled her while the big guy to her right pushed. She fell out of the car. They dragged her to the side entrance of the building and unlocked a padlock. They opened the door and threw her inside into the darkness.

The door slammed behind her. The padlock clicked shut. And all she could see were slivers of light seeping in through cracks in the corrugated-steel panels that were the building's walls.

It was taking forever for her eyes to adjust to the darkness. In the meantime, something scraped across the floor nearby.

7

UNWILLING DONORS

Okay, *now* was the time to get her magick on.

The first thing she did was cast a protection spell upon herself. Over the years, she'd learned how to do this quickly, but it required a great deal of energy.

She blocked out the noise from the darkness, controlled her panic, and dove deep into her innermost core to gather all the energy within herself and concentrate it, like packing snow into a snowball (on the one occasion in her life that she encountered snow). She also gathered what energy she could from the earth beneath the concrete floor and from the air itself.

That's all she had time for. She intoned the words of the spell while grasping her power amulet, the small pouch she kept in her pocket the kidnappers missed when they took her phone.

Soon, she sensed the invisible wall form around her. Right now, it would stop a lunging body, human, animal, or monster. But she would need to pump more energy into it to stop bullets and other projectiles.

Instead, she created an illumination orb, which was easy for her to do. The little floating ball of modest light was handy at night while camping or when searching for something in the back of a cabinet.

Now, it had a much different urgency.

The light rose seven feet in the air. It illuminated a small section of the floor and revealed a man standing there. He had a mullet haircut, a dirty tank top that rose on his flabby stomach to reveal his bellybutton, and torn jeans.

"Lookie here," he said. "We got us some company."

Instead of being relieved the guy wasn't a ghoul or something, she tensed even more at the last thing he said. Was she going to be attacked by a gang of depraved redneck men?

"I hope she's more intelligent than you," said a woman with a Spanish accent. A short, middle-aged woman moved into the pool of light. "Welcome to our prison."

"Yeah, welcome," several voices murmured behind them.

Missy moved the light orb toward the voices. Five adults, men and women ranging from their late-twenties to sixties, sat on the concrete floor, leaning back against the wall.

"How the heck are you doing that with the light?" the guy with the mullet asked.

"It's a little flashlight drone," Missy lied. "Why are we all here?"

"We call this the kidney farm," the Hispanic woman said.

"What do you mean?" Missy asked, though she had an inkling of the answer. With her mother, always assume the worst. Then make it a few notches worse than that.

"We're here to donate our kidneys," the woman explained. "Unwillingly. I answered an online ad for a housecleaner. When

I showed up at the house, two guys threw me into an SUV and took me here."

"I answered an ad for an arborist," the man with the naked bellybutton said. "I didn't know what an arborist was, though. I thought it said 'arsonist.' Anyway, turns out they didn't really want either one."

"It's the same with these other folks," the woman gestured toward the five people against the wall. "They answered fake ads and ended up here."

"How do you know they want your kidneys?" Missy asked.

"The doctor told us. I think he's a doctor. He looks like one. He wears a white lab coat covered with blood stains. He asked us lots of health questions. Then, each day, he takes one of us into another room. We never see them again."

So typical of her mother, Missy thought. Too impatient and immoral to do things the proper way, she had to illegally harvest kidneys from powerless people. Why did she need so many? The kidneys the "doctor" had removed must have been incompatible. Or maybe he just botched the procedure for removing them.

And it's soon going to be my turn. I should have sounded more enthusiastic on the phone about giving her a kidney.

"How long have you guys been here?" Missy asked.

"Me and Jimbo have been here more than a week," the Hispanic woman said. "The people back there arrived more recently. Some of them yesterday."

"How often does the doctor show up?"

"Almost every day."

"He brings a cooler," Jimbo said. "At first I thought it was his lunch. Then I figured out what it was for."

"They took away all your phones, right?"

Everyone nodded.

Missy had confidence her magick could help her break out of the building and free the other prisoners. But they were in the middle of nowhere, with no transportation. The bad guys could easily recapture them all as they wandered down the country roads in broad daylight.

"What time does the doctor usually come?" Missy asked.

Tires crunched the dirt parking lot outside. Two car doors opened and slammed.

Uh-oh.

Everyone in the room tensed and withdrew to the farthest, darkest corners, where they crouched, quivering.

Now I know what bait feels like when the giant hand reaches into the bucket for the next one headed to the hook.

A metal exterior door opened and closed in a distant part of the building. Then another door opened, sending a shaft of light into the room where the prisoners were.

"Hello, my little chickadees," a man with an Eastern European accent said as he entered the room. He wore blue scrubs, which, thankfully, were not splattered with blood.

He was followed by a giant man, also in scrubs, with blond hair who dwarfed the big guy who captured me.

"Oh, I see we have a new guest," the doctor said, appraising Missy. "And what blood type are you, my dear?"

Uh-oh.

"I wouldn't know."

"I cannot wait to find out. But first, I have other matters to attend to."

Missy breathed a sigh of relief when it seemed she wouldn't be the next minnow plucked from the bait bucket. Then, she realized one of the others would go under the knife.

Were they given proper care after their kidney was removed? What, exactly, happened to each prisoner who was taken away from this room to never return?

"Marta?" The doctor shined a flashlight around the room until he caught the middle-aged Hispanic woman in its beam. "Oh, there you are. Please come with us."

"No," Marta said in a low voice filled with dread.

"It won't hurt a bit, Marta. You'll be back on your feet in no time."

The doctor nodded to the huge blond guy. The giant strode across the floor toward Marta. Instead of cowering against the wall, she stood and shook her fist at the mass of muscle headed toward her.

"You leave my kidneys alone," the diminutive woman warned, though her brave facade was crumbling.

Jimbo stepped in front of Marta. "Wait," he said to the blond man.

The giant threw a roundhouse punch into Jimbo's jaw. Jimbo dropped to the floor.

Marta's eyes widened in surprise as the giant collapsed on the floor, too. He began snoring loudly, his head resting on Jimbo's gut as if it were a pillow.

The doctor's clipboard clattered upon the concrete floor. He leaned backwards against the wall and slid down it until he lay crumpled in a heap.

Missy's sleep spell worked as well as always.

"What happened?" Marta asked.

"They had heavy lunches and needed a little nap," Missy said. "Search their pockets for the car keys and let's get out of here."

Missy knelt beside Jimbo, checked his pulse, and opened his

eyelids to make sure his pupils weren't dilated. He seemed fine and was already returning to consciousness.

Earlier, Missy had planned, and dreaded, using her magick to try to open the padlock outside the door she had been thrown through when she arrived here. She knew several unlocking spells but struggled with them all.

Fortunately, the inner door the doctor and his stooge had come through remained unlocked. It led to what used to be an office but was now set up as an improvised operating room with a dirty table. Missy shuddered at the thought of having her kidney removed here. An exterior door led to the rear of the packing building where a black pickup truck sat.

She and Marta searched the room, the empty desk drawers, and cabinets. Her cellphone wasn't there, nor was anyone else's.

Missy had a dilemma. Should she use the doctor's phone, if she could unlock it, to call the police and let them handle it as the crime of kidnapping? What her mother had done involved no black magic. For once, this was a crime she had committed that could be prosecuted in a court of law.

But Missy didn't have time to deal with all the police interviews and court appearances. She wanted to investigate a demon summoning. And prevent a vampire-dragon war.

"Marta, please drive me to the nearest bus station," Missy said. "And then, return here and call the police."

"I don't know. Some of the others won't want that. They don't have their papers."

"Okay, then give those people rides home."

"Will I get in trouble for driving a stolen truck?"

"I'll make sure the two men stay asleep long enough for you to drop everyone off and return here. Then, please call the police, and report that you and Jimbo were abducted."

Marta nodded. "Tell me how you did that," she said.

"What?"

"Made them go to sleep."

"Just a little trick I learned along the way."

It turned out to be a good thing she hadn't used her sleep spell when she was kidnapped. Otherwise, she wouldn't have been able to free these people.

Magick can be a force of good even when you don't use it.

SHE RODE the bus to San Marcos. Then, she took a cab from the bus station to the beach where she'd left her car. The sun had set, and the parking lot was nearly empty.

Thankfully, her car was still there. And her phone lay on the floor in front of the driver's seat. One of the thugs who seized her must have tossed it there.

She made it to Bob's surf shop before it closed. Bob was sitting at the desk in the back room with Florence perched on his shoulder. They glanced at her with curiosity, but not guilty expressions.

"Did you tell my mother that I was here?"

"No," Bob said. "Like, why would I do that?"

"What about you?" Missy asked Florence with a stern glare.

The parrot squawked. "I don't want anything to do with that hag."

"Then, how would she know I was here? She even knew what part of the beach I was on."

"Dude, you're a smarter witch than that. Obviously, she's got, like, some sort of surveillance spell on you."

"I checked myself carefully before I left home. I was clean of outside magic."

"Maybe, she had a spell that was triggered when you came to San Marcos. Did you check yourself after you got here? Duh?"

"Um, no."

Missy stepped aside to the far corner of the workshop. Clearing her mind, she recited the words that made her consciousness self-reflective, then scanned for foreign energies.

Sure enough, some unfamiliar magic was observing her.

While she was still in a semi-trance state, she assembled a warding spell, a variation of the protection spell. The warding worked specifically to keep magic, rather than physical objects, from penetrating a sphere created around her.

When she was finished, she felt lighter and freer.

"Okay," she said, "problem solved."

Florence made an exact imitation of human snickering. Or maybe it was the real thing.

"I apologize for the accusatory tone," Missy said. "Being kidnapped makes me a little edgy."

"Whoa," Bob said. "What happened?"

Missy told the story.

"That woman sure wants a kidney," Bob said.

"Ideally, one of mine. That's why I wanted to know, for sure, if she killed my father."

"And she tried to take away your ability to decide."

"Stealing a kidney is the easiest way to get one for her, I guess. Only, the other kidneys must not have been compatible. Why didn't she use the regular healthcare system like everyone else, instead of that quack doctor?"

"Dude, black magic is about breaking the rules. Every kind of rule: physics, morality, religion. And common sense."

"I'm sure there must be a witch somewhere powerful enough to heal her through white magic," Missy said. "Right?"

"Not in our Guild. Healing is great, and all, but you can only go so far before you cross the line, you know? Depends on how close to dying the patient is. If a magician tries to act like God, then they're acting like Satan. Whoa, that was such a mind-blowing thing I just said!"

MISSY CALLED Matt and asked him to inquire about the kidnapping of the people at the orange-packing facility. He said there was no record of any case involving Ophelia Lawthorne, AKA Ruth Bent. There was a case involving a doctor and his assistant who kidnapped people to sell their kidneys on the black market. But there was no other defendant. Somehow Ophelia had managed to distance herself from her organ-harvesting scheme. She escaped with clean hands once again.

MISSY WOULD HAVE to wait until the next day to look for Wendall. So, she called her cousin, Darla, who lived in San Marcos. She was one of several family members Missy didn't know even existed until she learned about her birth parents and a world that had been kept secret from her. This was partly a decision made by her adoptive parents. It was also because Ophelia Lawthorne was such a scandal for the family that much of Missy's family tree was nearly erased.

Darla's mother was Ophelia's sister. Their mother, Missy's grandmother, was the matriarch of the Chesswick line of witches. They all practiced white magick, except for Ophelia, who embraced the darkness not long after she married Ted Lawthorne.

Ophelia's descent into evil caused her to be banned from the Magic Guild, the city, and eventually, her family.

"You must stay at the Esperanza," Darla said of the bed-and-breakfast inn she ran. "I have plenty of vacancies. And since you're exploring the past, Mom will insist you come by for dinner."

"But she had no warning," Missy said.

"She always cooks enough for leftovers. She won't mind at all."

Missy picked up a bottle of wine and arrived at Sadie Chesswick's Victorian home only a few minutes late. She'd met Darla and her family before, after rescuing Darla's daughter, Sophie, who'd been sold to a clan of vampires by an addiction-recovery company. Sophie was there for dinner, as well.

"So, my sister has been in touch with you?" Sadie asked while she served dessert. Her head was surrounded by a nimbus of frizzy black hair, with a recent dye job, similar to Ophelia's style. "Did she ever do the right thing and meet you in person?"

"I've met her in person, but she wasn't doing the right thing. Unless that includes trying to kill me."

Everyone's mouth dropped open, except for Darla's. She already knew the stories.

"Let's just say my interests clashed with hers on a couple of occasions," Missy said. "She did not appreciate me getting in the way."

"And now, she wants one of Missy's kidneys," Darla said.

"Hmm. She was always the selfish one when we were children," Sadie said. "The spoiled younger daughter.

"You would even consider giving that woman a kidney?" Darla asked.

"Daughters always want their mothers' approval," Missy said.

Everyone laughed.

"I want to know if she killed my father," Missy said, staring intently at Sadie. She lowered her eyes.

Everyone stopped laughing.

"The authorities are the only ones who really believed it was a freak dishwasher accident," Missy said. "Most in the magic community believe a demon did it."

Sadie nodded.

"They claimed a demon-summoning went horribly wrong," she said.

"But why would Ted, a successful white witch, summon a demon?" Missy asked. "Why not his wife, the black-magic sorceress? That's what they do."

"Your parents had already separated by then," Sadie said. "Your mother was living in the Orlando area. To summon a demon, you need to be in the same location where you want the demon to appear."

"So, she traveled back to San Marcos to do it," Missy said.

Sadie shook her head. "The Magic Guild conducted an investigation and cleared her. She supposedly had an alibi that put her in Orlando at the time of death."

"Do you trust the investigation?" Missy asked.

Sadie's expression was pained. "I don't now. Please understand it was very awkward for me having a sister who was Public Enemy Number One. We weren't speaking at that point in our lives, but her evil put a stain on me. I became less active in the Guild. In magic. It had become uglier in my eyes."

"That's why it's just a hobby for you now?" Darla asked. "Because you were treated poorly by the Guild?"

"I didn't say I was treated poorly. I meant there was whispering behind my back. Warding spells cast when I was around. My sister revealed the dark side of magic. And she wasn't the only one in the Guild to be sympathetic to black magic. Some people will do whatever it takes to have more power. So, that's why I don't trust the conclusions of the investigators. I don't believe they were fully impartial."

Missy thought about that as she chewed her pecan pie.

"Who from the Guild might know more—whom I can talk to and trust? Is Wendall trustworthy?"

"I always thought of him as a good, wise wizard," Sadie said. "He's friendly with Arch Mage Bob, who I'm not a fan of. But I would say Wendall is a good bet. And he can point you to other sources."

After dessert, Missy had a cup of tea, knowing she should leave soon, lest she outstay her welcome. But she had one last question.

"What were they like, my mother and father?"

Sadie didn't expect the question, but she smiled.

"When they married, they were young, creative, and idealistic. They were like artists, theater people, musicians, wanting to devote their lives to an art they were passionate about, but having to take odd jobs to pay the bills. You don't go into magic to get rich. Well, not white magic, that is. I think financial pressure was what first turned my sister into the wrong path. And then, the power—she became addicted to it."

"Was she jealous of my father?"

"Not at first, but yes, once his abilities grew. He was very accomplished and attracted a following. Not an organized coven, but almost like groupies. Ophelia did not like that one bit. He grew much more powerful than her, and she discovered black magic gave her a faster path to such power."

"And money," Missy said. "She hires herself out to the highest bidder these days. It's sad."

Missy realized she had caused gloom to fall upon the evening.

"Sorry for being a party-pooper," Missy said. "I guess that's my special power."

"I don't know what went through my sister's head when she left you and your father," Sadie said. "But she had no choice about giving custody to Ted. The Magic Guild forbade her from bringing you when they banned her from the city and county. You can't have a child in the same house as black magic."

"I was in my crib in the other room when the demon killed my father."

The heavy silence that followed resulted from her special power.

8

WITCHES PER SQUARE MILE

S he spotted Wendall at the end of the pier, right after she paid her fee and passed through the turnstile. The lanky man with the wide-brimmed hat stood out clearly from all the dads and kids and fat guys without shirts. She marched past them, their coolers, and the cut bait. Anglers leaned over the railings, watching their lines in the water, observing where the seabirds were feeding, and, most of all, monitoring what their competitors on the pier were catching.

He immediately recognized her as she approached.

"Well, well, Ms. Mindle. A pleasure seeing you again," Wendall said with a genuine grin.

"Hi, Wendall. I hope you're well."

"I have been. Doctor found a few pre-cancerous moles because I'm out in the sun too much. I removed them with a simple spell."

"I'm glad. Our magic, white magick, is all about healing."

"Something tells me you're about to draw a contrast with black magic. Is your mother up to no good again?"

"As always. But I'm here to ask you about what she was up to in the past. I've heard hints she may have been the one who summoned the demon who killed my father."

Wendall turned away and began reeling in the line on one of his rods. "Wouldn't know about that."

Wendall had a long, craggy face with a lantern jaw clamped tight with thought. His eyebrows were white and his eyes slate-blue. He used to be one of the most famous wizards in Florida at his peak.

"Do you have confidence in the investigation that cleared her? Bob said there were some doubts about it."

He turned back to her, his eyes troubled. "I trusted it."

He said nothing while he reeled in the rest of his line and found an empty hook beneath a sliding sinker. He baited it with a live shrimp from a bucket and tossed it back into the ocean.

Missy wanted to push him to say more but stayed silent. Finally, he spoke again.

"The investigator was a smart man," he said.

"Bob told me some in the Guild back then practiced black magic."

"Black magic is like cancer. It spreads and metastasizes. The witches of the Guild responsible for finding and eliminating black magic in our territory sometimes got a little too close to what they were trying to root out. Once you dabble in black magic, it corrupts your soul."

"So, the investigator, who believed Ophelia's alibi that she was in Orlando, was corrupt?" Missy asked.

"I didn't say that. I believe he was an honest wizard."

"Is he still alive? Can I speak with him?"

"I think he is. He's in a nursing home called Wellbrook, west of town. Name's Tommy Albinoni. You can tell him I sent you."

"Thank you."

"And I'll give you one more name. Eliza-May Jenkins."

"Who's she?"

"At the time of the incident, she was a young witch-in-training. She was an acolyte of your father. Totally smitten by him, in fact. She spent a lot of time with him. Maybe she knows something useful. Maybe not."

"Do you know where to find her?"

"Not a clue, my dear. You might have to use some magic."

ACTUALLY, Missy used some Google. Eliza-May was an actor. She had dozens of commercials and low-budget films among her credits, but her mainstay was local and regional theater. Her name popped up in several recent productions at the San Marcos Playhouse, including one that was currently running. Missy could not find any personal contact information for the actor, aside from her social media pages. So, she decided to drop by the theater downtown.

She had hoped to wander in and find the actor doing whatever actors do when they're not on stage. But there was a matinee performance in progress. She knew she wouldn't be allowed backstage after the show, so she sat on a bench outside the theater. If she was lucky, Eliza-May would step out for some fresh air during the downtime before the evening performance.

Missy was lucky. After all the audience had exited the theater, a group of younger folks, who looked like stagehands, left. A little while later, a thin woman in casual clothes stepped out onto the sidewalk.

Missy recognized her instantly as Eliza-May. She was older than the headshots found on the internet, probably in her late sixties. And she'd definitely had some plastic surgery done. But she held herself with confidence and poise, with all the airs of a diva who could command attention on the stage. Even though the stage was in little 'ol San Marcos.

The actor squared her shoulders and headed down the street. Missy didn't know how to approach her without seeming like a crazed fan.

Half a block ahead, the actor entered a historic-looking tavern. Missy followed, waited a couple of minutes, then went inside.

When her eyes adjusted to the dark interior, she spotted Eliza-May in a booth with a tiny lamp and lampshade. Eliza-May returned the menu to a male server with her order.

Missy sat at the bar and ordered a cola.

"Excuse me," she said to the server as he passed by. "Could you please tell Ms. Jenkins her meal is on me?"

The server smirked, thinking Missy was a psycho-fan. "Sure."

He returned to the table, spoke to the actor, and nodded toward Missy. The actor smiled warily.

Missy walked over.

"Thank you so much, dear, but I cannot accept," the actor said. She had a southern accent and a flamboyant style like Blanche from *A Streetcar Named Desire*.

"Please, I insist. I'm not some crazed fan. I wanted to meet you because you once knew my father. My name is Missy, and he was Ted Lawthorne."

Eliza-May's eyes opened in shock. Missy didn't know if it was real or acting.

"You're Ted's daughter?"

Missy nodded. "After his death, I was raised by his cousin's family. I knew very little about Ted until recently."

Eliza-May struggled inwardly. Was she going to welcome Missy, or run away?

"Please sit down, dear."

Missy grabbed her soda and slid into the booth across from her.

"I didn't know you had survived," Eliza-May said. "There was a rumor at the time the demon had killed you, too."

"Who summoned the demon? They made it sound as if my father did it and lost control of the demon. But he would never do black magic. At least, that's the impression I have of him."

"You are correct. Ted disdained the black arts. He was a great man, your father. I practically worshipped him. He not only knew more magick than anyone else, but he also developed new spells. Healing spells and other beneficial magick."

"I suspect my mother summoned the demon to kill him," Missy said. "What do you think?"

"Of course, she was accused of it. She was the first person who came to my mind. But the Guild's internal investigators cleared her. To be honest, she wasn't the only witch or wizard secretly involved with black magic at the time. It's quite possible someone else summoned the demon."

"But why? Who else would want to kill my father?"

"A rival."

"A rival? It's not like my father was a drug lord. He was a witch. There weren't territories or profits to fight over. And being jealous of his abilities doesn't seem enough reason to kill him."

"A rival for my affection," Eliza-May said. "Jealous that I was in love with your father. I'm talking about my boyfriend."

"Oh, wow. I didn't expect for you to go there."

"I'm just speculating he may have done it. The possibility occurred to me after your mother was cleared of the crime."

"So were you and my father . . ."

"Intimate? Yes, but only after he separated from your mother."

"I never thought the Magic Guild would be so melodramatic," Missy said. "The only witches I know back home other than me are old crones and a real estate agent. No one's a rival. No one slays people with demons."

"Well, the more witches you have per square mile, the more melodrama there is. San Marcos is like Ground Zero for magicians. And those days back then were a golden age for magic."

"They don't sound so golden to me."

"It did get to be too much. That's why I left the field. I wanted an honest job. If you can call acting honest."

"You've completely given up magic?"

"Mostly, except for a few spells now and then, like when a fellow actor forgets his line. Or a stoplight is red for too long."

"Can I ask who this boyfriend was? And how to reach him? I want to talk to him, even if he's not honest with me."

"You can't talk to him," Eliza-May said.

"Why not?"

"He's dead. He was a much older man when we dated, and too many years have gone by since then."

"Oh. I'm sorry. Can I have his name, though?"

"No. I promised him I'd never divulge it."

Missy didn't know what to say.

The server arrived with Eliza-May's burger.

"It's okay if you don't want to pay for my meal anymore," the actor said.

"I still do. Every bit of information helps."

NEXT, she needed to speak with Tommy Albinoni, who had been the Guild's investigator. The Wellbrook Assisted Living facility was outside of town, in a leafy area just past a veterinarian and a landscaping store. The single-story brick structure looked old but well maintained.

As she pulled in and passed the sign for the facility, Missy's eye caught a strange symbol in the bottom corner. It was an emblem with the letters "MG." The public would have no idea what the symbol meant, but Missy knew it represented the Magic Guild.

So, this was a retirement center supported by the Guild. The folks living here were retired witches, wizards, and mages. Bingo Night must get really crazy, she thought.

The middle-aged woman at the front desk didn't seem like she had magic in her, but Missy's senses couldn't always be reliable in determining that.

"Could you please tell Tommy Albinoni that he has a visitor?" Missy asked. "A friend of a friend."

"Is he expecting you?"

"No, but I'll wait."

She sat in a plastic chair and did just that: waited. For an hour. What did Albinoni have to do that was so important he couldn't come see her? Macrame class?

During the excruciating wait, a group of residents walked by, headed outside. The women all used canes and seemed normal. Until they got outside, that is. One of them began levitating and chased a squirrel up a tree. Another waved her hands, and the clothing flew off a male landscape worker. The naked, muscular guy continued with his weed-whacking, oblivious to his nudity. The woman who had hexed his clothes off, was not oblivious to it at all.

About twenty minutes later, the front door opened on its own. Missy wondered what had caused it. Then, a case of beer floated into the building and headed down the hallway.

The front-desk worker cursed and ran after the beer, catching the case and carrying it back to the lobby. She dialed a number on the switchboard.

"Mr. Johnson, your doctor said no more drinking! Knock it off."

Finally, a male aide pushed a wizened man in a wheelchair down the main hallway.

"Are you Mr. Albinoni's visitor?" the aide asked.

"Yes," Missy said, standing. "Hello, Mr. Albinoni. I'm Missy Mindle."

"Yeah, what do you want?" the elderly man asked in a gruff voice with a hint of an Italian accent.

"My parents were Ted and Ophelia Lawthorne," she said, waiting to observe his reaction.

There was none.

"So what?"

"You oversaw the Guild's investigation of my father's death. You ruled it murder by a demon."

"Right. Asmodeus it was."

"Many in the Guild suspected my mother was the one who summoned the demon. You ruled her out. Why?"

"From what I remember, her alibi held up. She was too far away from the death scene to have controlled the demon."

"You simply took her word for it?"

"No, I corroborated it." He was angry. "I don't appreciate being accused of malfeasance. There was no wizard more concerned with integrity than me. Not just my personal integrity, but the Guild's, as well. We must be just and righteous. We must be impartial. Even the hint of not living up to those qualities completely erodes our authority. And then what do we have? A Guild must be trusted absolutely, or no one would follow its rules. We regulate the supernatural and paranormal, and people who study those arts are always pushing limits. How could we claim authority to regulate them if we're seen as biased and corrupt?"

"So, you're telling me I just need to trust you?" Missy asked.

"Yes! You have no respect for institutions. But you will when you're no longer young."

"I'm not young. I'm in my forties."

"You're a baby, young lady, to someone like me."

"Thank you. I guess."

"Well, go on about your business. I have nothing else to tell you."

"You know of no one who could have summoned the demon?"

"No. I didn't then, and I don't now. There is no forensic evidence when you summon a demon, aside from the paraphernalia you used in the ceremony. And that is almost worthless as hard evidence. Daniel, I am done with this interview. Please wheel me to the Pilates studio."

So, off he went, leaving Missy with nothing. Still, Albinoni was a bit too defensive. Maybe, there was more he hadn't told her.

`THE TEXT from Agnes was cryptic:

"Please return to Jellyfish Beach at once. The war has begun."

Missy drove straight to the Esperanza Inn, gathered her things, and checked out. She gave Darla a big hug.

"When will you come back?" Darla asked.

"Very soon. I still have several stones to uncover."

She threw her bag into her old Toyota, recited a spell to ensure it wouldn't break down, and headed toward a crisis of unknown dimensions.

9

PLAYING THROUGH

The foursome from Dearborn, Michigan, were the only humans on the golf course. The men, in town for a ball-bearing convention, were such atrocious players that six hours after they teed off, they still hadn't completed eighteen holes. What fooled them was the golf course's late closing time. They had believed this meant the course was lighted.

They were wrong. The course stayed open until 3:00 a.m. because it accommodated the vampire retirees in Jellyfish Beach, and vampires didn't need lights to see what they were doing. The owner of the club was a vampire, as were most of the club members. During the day, a small number of human players enjoyed an uncrowded course. They would leave before sundown. And then, the vampires would tee off.

Except tonight, the four Michiganders were still stumbling around in the darkness on the sixteenth green.

Until the stars were blotted out by immense dark shapes flying above.

"What the heck is that?" asked Fred Dwimblebutt, Senior Ball Bearing Sales Consultant. He pointed to a dark shape sweeping across the sky directly toward them.

"A bat?" asked his protege, Pablo Pascales.

"That's awfully big for a bat," said Doug Delish, Ball Bearing Design Director. "Of course, this is Florida, so I'm not surprised they have freakishly large bats."

"Maybe we should wrap this up," Billy Pickler whined. "I can't find my ball. Can't see a darned thing."

As if to answer his need, the green was illuminated by a great light. It was a gush of flames coming from the freakishly large bat's mouth.

The flames engulfed Billy Pickler. The last words he emitted in his earthly existence were:

"I don't think they're bats."

His coworkers scurried away in every direction. Doug Delish made it to an oak tree beside the next fairway. He wondered if he should follow the rules about avoiding lightning and trees. Instead, he followed the ancient primate ancestral instinct in his brain and jumped, grabbing the lowest limb of the tree, and pulled himself up, climbing the branches above until he was hidden. He survived.

Pablo Pascales sprinted toward the nearest water hazard. He dove into the pond and remained underwater, holding his breath.

He, too, survived the dragon attack. However, unbeknown to him, he shared the pond with a twelve-foot alligator. He survived the dragon, but not the gator.

Fred Dwimblebutt, who considered himself the smartest

guy of the foursome, made it to the golf cart. He zipped down the paved golf cart path toward the clubhouse. The path was the only part of the course illuminated at night.

Unfortunately for Billy, the lighting made him an easy target. Three dragons glided behind him, low to the ground. The dragons entertained themselves by seeing which one could get closest to their prey without knocking him off the path. Finally, they allowed the younger of the three to enjoy the easy pickings.

The dragon picked up the cart in his jaws. Being a younger dragon, he was fascinated by the high-pitched squeals the driver was making. The human gripped the steering wheel and repeatedly slammed the cart's brake, as if that would stop his ascent into the sky. The dragon watched him with one eye and giggled in a dragon's way. He wanted to play with his prize.

So, once he reached several hundred feet in altitude, he dropped the cart. He let it fall, then swooped down and caught it again. He did this several times until the human fell out of the cart and landed on the roof of the clubhouse. By then, the dragon had lost interest and dropped the cart upon the human. He flew after his companions to look for more prey.

The senior dragon of the group realized their first victims were humans, not vampires, but the distinction seemed irrelevant to a dragon. However, all the other humanoids spread out across the golf course were vampires. And among them was Bill.

Bill's game was rusty, because over the last hundred years he'd preferred to spend his time at the shooting range instead of the driving range. But he was talked into playing tonight by his friend, Stanley Gardiner, who was hosting Bill at his home. Stanley had invited him to stay at his community called Alligator Hammock, a fifty-five-plus retirement village west of town. It was the only other all-vampire community besides Squid Tower.

Bill didn't enjoy being a houseguest of Stanley and his wife. They wouldn't let him bring his weapons into the house. He had to keep them in the trunk of his car, only a fraction of his total arsenal. He couldn't wait until the vampires of Squid Tower accepted the righteousness of his war against the Reptilians and welcomed him back.

"Did you see that human falling from the sky?" Stanley asked while they were putting on the fourteenth green.

Bill glanced up as dark shadows flew by overhead. Flames shot from the shadows, and the vampire foursome playing ahead of them disappeared from the fifteenth tee.

"Get down!" Bill shouted. "It's Reptilians!"

Since he was playing golf, Bill was only lightly armed tonight. Besides his Glock 9 mm weapon of choice, he had a .45 Colt revolver, an electric stun baton, pepper spray, and a hunting knife. He felt vulnerable with so few weapons.

But before Stanley even hit the ground, Bill was in a firing stance, firing shot after shot with his Glock at the Reptilians overhead.

It got their attention. The three dragons circled and headed toward him.

Bill realized that standing in the middle of the green wasn't the safest defensive point. He jumped into a sand trap as jets of fire engulfed the fourteenth hole, just missing the prone figure of Stanley.

Bill found good cover beneath the lip of the bunker, put in a new clip, and continued firing as the dragons passed overhead.

The smaller one screamed a screeching, hissing wail. As they flew out of range, one dragon grabbed the young one with its talons to help keep it aloft.

Soon, the dragons disappeared into the night sky.

"No more waiting for the Reptilians to attack," Bill said, mostly to himself, since Stanley was still blubbering with fear. "It's time to go on the offensive."

BILL NEEDED an army to defeat the Reptilians. Oleg and Sol did not an army make. One or two other vampires at Squid Tower might be depended on to follow the call of duty. And there were surely a handful from Stanley's community who could be convinced to join. Even so, it was pretty pathetic. His Boy Scout troop back in 1912 was a more formidable force than this.

He would have to recruit others besides vampires. Perhaps the werewolves in the buildings next door, though he despised them. Perhaps regular humans, even. Florida had hordes of armed humans, many of whom were already in a militia of some sort. It shouldn't be too difficult to raise an army of humans. Actually, more of a special forces unit like a Seal team. Led by vampires, of course. Vampires who didn't let on that they were vampires.

Bill was certain he was destined for this task. He'd spent his later years as a human, and all his years as a vampire, regretting that he hadn't joined the military when he was young. Of course, back then, he was more of a wimp—not the fearless warrior he was today.

He was a late bloomer, for sure. But now, he had reached the pinnacle of his existence. It was time to fulfill his destiny and save the planet from a sinister enemy.

And it would be fun, too. Just the thought of how much ammo he'd go through got his undead heart racing at three beats a minute.

There was a gun show at the Crab County Fairgrounds this weekend, beginning Friday night after sunset. The place would be overflowing with patriots. Well-armed ones, at that.

At first Bill considered paying for an exhibitor table if it wasn't too late to do so. He could sit there and hand out pamphlets about the Reptilians and have a sign-up sheet for his special forces unit.

But he discarded this idea. He imagined most of the people stopping at his table would be the kinds of attendees who methodically work their ways through the tables without any real aim or objective. It would be a waste of time and money.

No, he wanted people who were already believers in the Reptilians, who were deeply concerned about them. Men (Bill was too old-fashioned to even imagine women warriors) who were ready to make the commitment to fight back.

So, on Friday night, Bill bought his ticket to the show and, once inside, deployed his recruitment tactic: sandwich board signs. His front and back were covered by foam-core boards with the famous image of Uncle Sam pointing at you from a World War I poster. Bill had written the message: "I want YOU to fight the Reptilians."

It was a brilliant idea that actually worked. Even though he stood off to the side of the entrance with guys holding signs that said, "Jet contrails turn you gay," and "Gravity is only a theory," Bill had many people approach him.

Every few minutes, a different man would ask what he could do to fight the dastardly aliens. All the men were self-selected candidates, already deeply immersed in the conspiracy theory, armed, and eager to use those arms.

By the time the show closed for the night, everyone had left, and the security guards ordered Bill to leave, he had over two hundred email addresses. He figured a third to a half of these men would come through and sign up.

He named his army ERR: Earthlings Resisting Reptilians. Soon, training would begin. And shortly afterwards, their hour of glory would arrive.

"I DON'T UNDERSTAND why we only train at night," said Abe, the African-American former Special Forces sergeant.

"My observation is the Reptilians are most active at night," Bill replied.

Bill had assigned Abe as the commander of the human contingent of the ERR Army. They were the twenty-three humans who showed up to the first two meetings, out of the 232 who had given their email addresses to Bill at the gun show. That left four vampires: Sol, Oleg, Stanley, and himself. The trick was hiding the fact the vampires were vampires, while building unit cohesion between the living and the undead.

"I think we should train in daylight, as well," Abe said. "Soldiers need to be ready to fight twenty-four-seven."

"Um, good idea, Sergeant. The senior members will undergo different training during daylight hours."

"You mean you old, pasty-white guys? What's the deal with that creepy one with the pointy ears?"

"Sol is a good soldier. Don't judge him by his looks."

Bill was reluctant to admit he was intimidated by Abe. Not only did Abe have a real military background, unlike Bill, he was aggressive and frequently challenged Bill's authority. Bill had to face the fact that he and the vampires were elderly weekend warriors. Except for Oleg, they weren't actual soldiers, compared to the ex-military and ex-law enforcement members who, along with the crazy extremists, constituted ERR.

And Oleg seemed to resent Bill for assuming senior command. But Oleg had fought in the days of muskets. He didn't appreciate modern military hardware as much as Bill.

Bill and his fellow vampires could keep up (almost) during the drills, because their vampire superpowers overcame the geriatric bodies in which they were trapped, since they were turned years ago. But they had to accept the fact they had become soft. The mellow, pleasure-filled retirement lifestyle, with the nightly visits of the Blood Bus if they didn't feel like hunting, had lost them their edge. They didn't have the blind courage of someone like Abe, or Tony, the insane former bank robber who wanted to kill cops as much as Reptilians.

Endless nights sipping pint bags of blood by the swimming pool had stripped Bill of his homicidal instincts. Or maybe he never had any to begin with.

He'd have to work on fixing that.

THE FIRST REAL mission of the ERR Army was a night search-and-destroy patrol in the Everglades. Bill was painfully aware that he didn't know how to find the Reptilians, but they could find him. And they were able to disappear through invisible portals to return to their home planet.

In essence, Bill's strategy was to patrol areas where he'd seen Reptilians before, and hopefully draw them out to attack the army. Then, the aliens would be destroyed.

It didn't begin so well.

The army marched together as one unit. Oleg pointed out that this was a bad strategy, but Bill and Abe didn't want to split their force into smaller teams until they could measure its performance in the swamps, prairies, and mangrove wetlands of the landscape.

After only thirty minutes of marching along a dirt road, gunfire erupted from the point of the column. Bill and Abe rushed up to see what happened.

"Bagged me a Reptilian, I sure did," said a bearded guy named Lucius. He wasn't ex-military. And he'd been booted out of every militia he'd joined.

"That's not a Reptilian," Abe said. "It's an alligator."

"It's a reptile, is what it is," said Lucius.

"Right. A reptile, not a Reptilian."

"Lucius, didn't you watch my presentation about Reptilians?" Bill asked.

"Guess I fell asleep during that one."

"Remember," Bill said, "they look like very tall humans with strange eyes. When they're in full reptile mode, they look like dragons."

"Got it," Lucius said.

The march continued. Bill didn't expect they would find Reptilians on every mission. They needed to be patient. He'd explained that in his presentation.

Fifteen minutes later, a clamor arose from the rear of the column. Bill and Abe rushed back there to see what happened.

Four skinny twenty-something males stood in their underwear with their hands in the air. They were shaking with fear. Eight ERR members surrounded them with rifles aimed.

"We got ourselves some Reptilians," said an anti-government militia member named Red. "Look how tall they are."

"Actually, we're Norwegian," said the tallest captive.

His accent sounded Norwegian, Bill believed. He looked kind of Norwegian, too.

"We are here fishing and camping," the captive explained. "But these guys just dragged us out of our tents."

"I don't think they're Reptilians," Bill said.

"Reptilians blend into our society," Red insisted.

"Did you sleep through my presentation?"

"No. You showed drawings of what they look like in their natural form. You showed us pictures of dragons. And you showed us photos of some of the famous people who are really Reptilians, like two ex-presidents, the Pope, and a 1980s hair-metal band. They all looked like normal people. Like our prisoners."

"Reptilians infiltrate the highest levels of society," Bill said. "They don't go camping in a mosquito-infested swamp."

"Then what the heck are *we* doing here?"

"You really didn't pay attention to my presentation. I put a lot of time into building those charts and graphs. What I said in the presentation was the Everglades is a crossroads where the Reptilians come in and out of our world. They're travelling through here. Not camping in tents."

"This stuff is too complicated," Red said.

"That's why you need to spend more time on the internet learning about conspiracies. It makes you much smarter. Let these people go."

"Wait," Abe said. "I want to check one thing I learned on the internet."

He walked to the nearest Norwegian and yanked down his boxer shorts. Everyone turned their heads away.

"Oh, sorry. Yeah, they're not Reptilians. Let them go."

"Sorry," Bill called out as the embarrassed and annoyed Norwegians hurried back to their campsite.

"These guys need more training," Abe said to Bill.

"I could give my presentation again."

"Maybe spice it up a little this time. And not as many slides."

Movement caught his eye. The troops were at the southern point of the Everglades on the shore of Florida Bay. A belt of mangrove trees lined the shoreline to their west.

The air was shimmering just in front of it. Bill could see it clearly with his vampire vision. Even the guys who had night-vision goggles didn't seem to notice.

Something slipped out of the shimmering section of air and crawled into the cover of the mangroves. Bill sprinted toward it.

He reached the mangroves and stepped into calf-deep water to get around the tangled roots. Through the branches, he saw the creature scurrying away from him. But he plunged through the narrow trees, slipping on their underground roots, diving forward to tackle it.

He held it in his arms as it squirmed to get away, scraping him with its claws. He stood, the small dragon firmly in his grasp. It weighed thirty or forty pounds, like a medium-sized dog. But much stronger.

"Calm down. I've got you."

A small blast of flame shot from the creature's nostrils and burned some leaves.

To the average person, it would look like a baby dragon. But Bill knew what it really was.

"It's a baby Reptilian," he shouted to the troops. "Yes! We have a hostage. They'll surely do what we say now that we have one of their babies. This, gentlemen, could turn the tide of the war."

"YOUR DRAGON FRIEND CONTACTED ME," Agnes said on the phone as Missy drove back to Jellyfish Beach. "He spoke to me telepathically."

"Yeah, he enjoys doing that."

"He said his daughter was captured by an army of militant humans and vampires."

"Oh, my. Bill has been busy."

"Yes, he's organized a militia of other nut jobs like himself. All heavily armed, from what Oleg told me."

"Oleg is with them?"

"Not anymore. He and Sol continued to play soldier with Bill, even after he disrupted the parley with Ronnie. But Oleg said they quit the militia after what just happened. He said they're all a bunch of idiots, and now that they have a hostage, things could go very badly."

"What did Ronnie say?"

"He said things will go very badly. Especially if he doesn't get his daughter back unharmed."

"Oh, my."

"I don't know why a young dragon would be on her own at a time like this," Agnes said.

"She probably wasn't alone. She was most likely part of a

group, including adults, traveling together. I'm guessing Bill came upon the young dragon just as she was passing through a gateway."

"Regardless of what happened, we need to put a stop to this. Both dragons and vampires have been lost. Some humans, too, from what I've heard. Now, this incident will cause a major escalation."

Missy spent the rest of the drive trying to reach Ronnie telepathically. Which was difficult since she wasn't a telepath. He must have sensed her efforts, because when she was about an hour outside of Jellyfish Beach, words entered her head. They were in Ronnie's voice with its slight Southern accent.

Get me my daughter back now.

Ronnie, please let's talk, she replied in her head. But he didn't answer.

How could she get a bunch of hotheads to listen when they were itching for a fight?

She would have to do something extremely risky.

REPTILE REVOLT

Sol and Oleg lay on sun loungers near the swimming pool, moon-bathing. It was a pleasant night, and the pool wasn't crowded. Sol smoked a fat cigar, shirtless and in a bathing suit that was bright red against his pale-as-death skin. He hadn't felt this relaxed in ages.

"This is what retirement is about," Oleg said.

"You got that right," Sol replied. "I worked as a clerk for forty-five years. Back in those days, in the sixteen hundreds, retirement had a different meaning. It just meant you were too old to work. You suffered in poverty until you croaked. Unless your kids were doing well enough to take you in and feed you."

"It was the same when I was human," Oleg said.

"When my eyes started to go kaput on me, I knew my days were numbered. It was like a death sentence. Little did I know I was going to be turned into a vampire, my meager savings would grow from compound interest over the centuries, and I would end up buying an oceanfront condo in Florida. It ain't the most luxurious community, but Squid Tower sure beats the streets of South Boston where I would've starved to death as an old man."

"I know what you mean," Oleg said, still with his heavy Russian accent despite being in America for over a hundred years.

"And we almost ruined it all by falling under the spell of Bill," Sol said. "What were we thinking?"

"When I saw the men he recruited, I knew we were in trouble," Oleg said. "There was no discipline, no standards. Even the men who had served in the military acted like sociopaths."

"That's for sure. It was a motley crew, all right. But what the heck happened to Bill? I always thought he was a kook, but he's gone off the deep end with all his weapon hoarding. And now, this thing with the Reptilians? I'm sorry, but I just don't buy it."

"I do not believe it either. I couldn't even if I tried. The reason I went along was a sense of solidarity with my vampire friends."

"Same here. Sure, I like to shoot a gun now and then. But who wants to spend the evening with a bunch of thugs who think they're Rambo and want to take down the government?"

"When I saw that baby dragon, I was finished with Bill. Any idiot could see it was a dragon, not an imaginary Reptilian. That baby has a very angry mother. We could have ended up torched to death like Marvin."

Sol sat up and looked at Oleg. "You really think that's how he died? From a dragon?"

"Well, after the dragon came here and torched Bill's balcony, I believed that's what happened to Marvin."

"I don't believe that. Nope. I think Bill killed Marvin."

"You do?" Oleg asked, incredulous. "And you still joined his militia?"

"I didn't really mind him killing Marvin. I hated Marvin."

"Yeah. So did I."

"But that doesn't change the fact that Bill locked him on his balcony and let him get sun-torched. I used to hear them arguing all the time. And Bill is definitely cold-blooded enough to do it. What I don't understand, is why he took up Marvin's Reptilian conspiracy theory."

"Yes, exactly. If what you say is true, he eliminated a lunatic only to become one himself."

"And now, a dragon is probably going to eliminate Bill. To paraphrase an American expression, the reptiles have come home to roost."

"There is a similar expression in Russian." Oleg said it in his native tongue, though it was complete gibberish to Sol.

"To paraphrase," Oleg said, "the squashed salamander once believed he was so smart."

"Good one," Sol said, puffing on his cigar. "Good one."

RONNIE, the dragon, was the Anointed One, according to dragon mystics. Ever since his species was driven off the planet by humans wearing armor, dragons have dreamed of reclaiming their glory. Centuries upon centuries of hiding in vast wilderness areas and escaping to the In Between for safety allowed their numbers to increase.

As humans developed sophisticated weaponry, the dragons knew they faced much more dangerous adversaries than knights. If dragons were ever to regain their status as apex predators, they would need a great dragon to lead them against a human species with effective ways of wiping them out again.

Ronnie was believed to be the great one his species has waited for. Already, he had proven the ability to shape-shift, which was rare among dragons. And ever since adolescence, other species of reptiles showed reverence for him.

The common household geckos and anoles of Florida used variations of their courtship behavior—pushups and pulsing throats—to worship him. The same with iguanas. Even alligators would appear when Ronnie was near a body of water, arrange themselves in a circular formation, and hold their mouths open wide for him.

At first, Ronnie merely found this amusing. But as the belligerent humans pushed the dragons into war, Ronnie devised a total-war strategy.

When his daughter was captured, he turned it up several notches. And sent his magical commands into the world.

FIRST CAME THE IGUANAS. They were stealthy, hiding in trees and on canal banks. But as they assembled in greater and greater numbers, South Florida homeowners viewed them with alarm. They called wildlife hotlines and were ignored. Their landscaping services went after them with machetes. The small number of iguanas who died were considered martyrs by their brethren.

All at once, on a Tuesday at 10:30 a.m., a date and time that was significant only to the reptile brain, the iguanas attacked.

No, they didn't directly attack humans. They're not that kind of reptile. Instead, they ate every single flower in every flower bed. Home vegetable gardens disappeared. Yards were burrowed into and destroyed.

And the iguanas pooped in swimming pools. They do this regularly anyway, but under the mass hypnosis that made them gather in suburbia to do battle, they pooped on an industrial scale. By 5:00 p.m. on that fateful Tuesday, henceforth known as The Day of the Iguana, every swimming pool in South Florida had become a murky iguana toilet.

And the lizards didn't stop there. They had conquered the suburban yards, but next, they invaded the homes.

Thousands of frantic emergency calls came in as iguanas popped up in toilets. Iguanas showed up in washing machines, bathtubs, bidets. Even in hot tubs, and several human swingers were rushed to the hospital with heart attacks.

No people died as a direct result of an iguana attack. The human casualties resulted when people scurried away from the lizards and fell off their patios or backed into the path of a car. Technically, it was their own fault, not that of the iguanas.

What the iguanas accomplished was to send a message to humans: you can kill us and even use us in enchilada recipes. But we own this place now. We're not a native species, but neither are you, humans. And we're in charge now.

The vampires of Squid Tower and Alligator Hammock received the same treatment as the humans. The most dangerous predators of humans, the undying vampires freaked out when they found an iguana in their toilet bowl.

And the iguanas were just the beginning.

ALL ROY WANTED WAS a peaceful day of fishing. He hoped to catch a couple of bass, or at least some bluegill or crappie. Most of all, he wished to sit in his little johnboat beneath the shade of a tree and see the leaves reflected on the placid lake. To eat his pimento cheese sandwich, sip some iced tea, and let the stress flow from his body, through the rod and line, and out into the water.

That's all he desired for his day off from caring for Ellie, hidden deep beneath her cloak of dementia. Relaxation was all he asked for. Heck, he didn't really care if he caught any fish. He wanted to imagine it was thirty years ago when he would fish this same lake with Ellie in the other seat of this same johnboat.

But the boys from town had other designs.

They came like a swarm of angry bees. Jet Skis. Six of them carrying young punks who cared nothing about the lake, the beautiful surroundings, or the biodiversity of the ecosystem. The lake could be a road as far as they were concerned. They wanted speed and the rush of jumping each other's wakes.

Their motors roaring, they came from the boat ramp on the opposite side of the lake. Traveling in a corkscrew pattern, they buzzed the boats fishing on the lake, which were spaced far apart to show courtesy.

The Jet Skis showed no respect at all, spraying the fishermen with their wakes as they passed dangerously close.

They came for Roy next. He didn't understand why they wanted to invade the little cove where he was anchored, unless part of the fun for the young men was the annoyance they caused others.

They made a beeline for his boat. He braced for a collision. With only feet to spare, each Jet Skier did a sharp one-eighty and buzzed away, sending waves of water into Roy's boat.

One after another, six Jet Skis in all, played this one-way game of chicken with Roy.

His head throbbed from fear and anger. His face was wet from the spray.

"Get out of here, you punks!" he shouted.

One of them flipped him the bird.

The personal watercraft raced from the cove. But then, they circled and headed back toward Roy.

Except, this time it was different.

One by one, they entered the cove.

And one by one, each driver was tackled by a gator leaping out of the water.

Yes, leaping into the air like they do at the alligator farms during the feeding shows for tourists—using their powerful tails to rocket upward and chomp their jaws on the chickens dangled by the handlers.

Today, however, it was Jet-Ski-riding punks the gators chomped their jaws upon. The gators knocked the punks from their crafts and fell back into the water, dragging their prey into the depths.

One by one, the humans disappeared. And one by one the riderless Jet Skis, engines cut off by the safety cords, sloshed into the bank of the cove beneath the trees.

Bubbles rose to the surface and burst. But neither the gators nor the humans came up again.

Roy bailed out his boat with a small plastic bucket. He took a long drink of iced tea. He sighed, letting the stress flow out of his shoulders, to his fishing rod, then down the line and into the lake where, down there somewhere, the gators prepared to feast.

Ah, Roy thought, peace and quiet. At last.

THE REPTILES and amphibians of Florida were rising up under the spell of the dragon king, the Anointed One, king of the kings of reptiles.

In some cases, there were small acts of rebellion, such as the handler at the alligator feeding show, who got yanked from his ladder instead of the chicken. Or the alligator wrestler performing in the Everglades park, who lost his face to his usually docile partner.

You know the freaky guy with the white hair and tattoos who shows up at the public beach in Jellyfish Beach, wrapped by his pet Boa constrictor, and poses for pictures with tourists?

He is no longer with us. Horrified tourists witnessed his demise, and videos of it went viral.

The little lizards every homeowner has, the green anoles outside on the patio, and the geckos who sneak inside and show up on the bathroom wall, were part of the uprising, too. They had a harder time than their larger comrades in taking out humans. But it was amazing how well tiny, unintelligent creatures can cooperate when under the magical influence of their mighty ruler.

It doesn't take much to make a human slip on the pool deck or in the bathtub. A human sleeping with his mouth open only requires a few brave lizards to block his airway. And drivers discovered the only things more deadly than other Florida drivers are hordes of geckos appearing from beneath the car seat and swarming over your face when you're trying to negotiate I-95.

Many Florida reptiles and amphibians didn't need to go to great lengths to take out humans. Many of them were already deadly to begin with. Such as the pygmy rattlesnakes hiding beneath the bags of mulch outside the home-improvement store. The humans loading up their carts with forty-pound bags normally aren't prepared to dodge rattlesnake strikes.

Even Cane, or "Bufo," Toads, the invasive creatures nearly as large as dinner plates, joined in the act. They are notorious for the glands on their backs that secrete poison when harassed by predators such as the family dog. It took true toad ingenuity to find a way to poison humans, too. But humans often aren't much brighter than toads. Especially. when they place their cold beverages down beside the swimming pool and take their eyes off them long enough for the toads to hop by.

The human casualties added up while society remained unaware of a pattern behind all these freak accidents. But what about the vampires? How did the dragon king attack these monsters who sleep during the day when most reptiles are active?

It turns out reptiles are far more cunning than you'd imagine.

On Tuesday evening, around midnight, Evie Gaynor was taking a moonlight dip in the ocean. Sharks usually don't bother swimmers, except by accident when pursuing fish. Undead vampires are even more unappetizing to sharks.

The American crocodile, which can be found in South Florida and Central America, lives in saltwater and is active at night. It's not known for attacks against humans or vampires. However, when under the spell of the ruler of all reptiles, it will prey upon anything it is commanded to.

Various parts of Evie washed up in the tide the next morning. Even vampires can't heal themselves when they're in several pieces. A man taking an early morning walk on the beach reported finding a woman's head wearing a bathing cap. When the sun came over the horizon, nothing was left but a bathing cap full of ashes. The police did not believe the man's tale about a woman's head.

George Martelli, a vampire since the seventeenth century, was not afraid of rats or spiders. But he was very afraid of geckos. A neighbor heard his scream and glass breaking. George was found impaled by a glass shard through his heart after he fell through his sliding-glass door.

As mentioned earlier, iguanas have an uncanny knack at showing up in toilet bowls. But never have hundreds come out of a single toilet before. Until Tuesday afternoon, when Cindy Shatmeyer ran screaming onto her balcony where she was promptly sun-torched.

When a neighbor went to check on her, the hundreds of iguanas scurried from Cindy's condo and chased the neighbor to the stairwell, down the stairs, and across the lobby, until the neighbor ran outside and experienced Cindy's fate next to the shuffleboard courts.

Only a direct attack by dragons could devastate the vampire population, but these attacks were psychologically damaging. They sent the message that the natural world had declared war on Squid Tower and Alligator Hammock.

"We have to do something," Agnes told the Board and Missy. "We must return the baby dragon to its parents before more of us are lost."

Even Schwartz, who was indifferent to the suffering of others, had been shaken.

"I hate snakes," he said. "There better not be any snakes in my condo. Ever."

"We must stop this insane war," Agnes said.

NEXT DOOR to Squid Tower was Seaweed Manor, another fifty-five-plus retirement community built in the late 1960s. All the residents were werewolves. Some of them were a bit on the rough side, and it wasn't uncommon to see the shifters get a little too rowdy on a full moon, drink a little too much before shifting, and get into vicious fights over dominance issues.

But largely, the residents were peaceful. They rarely devoured humans, preferring small wild game, if they still hunted at all.

They had no conflict with the dragons. It's doubtful any of the werewolves knew they existed. But, being humanoid, the werewolves were considered an enemy by the reptiles and amphibians that revolted against two-legged species.

Among the Seaweed Manor residents who still hunted were those who belonged to the Werewolf Women's Club. This community group, when not having bake sales or bridge tournaments, loved to go on outings to hunt and eat possums.

The timing of this year's Everglades Hunt and Picnic couldn't have been more unfortunate.

The ladies assembled at a picnic pavilion decked out in their finest outdoor-themed outfits. Their president, Josie Denton, sported a safari outfit with a wide-brimmed hat worn at a jaunty tilt.

"Ladies," she said, "Emma and Cindy will now present this year's gift for each of you. Hand-quilted dog beds! If you ever want to take a nap while in wolf form. Aren't they cozy looking?"

The two-dozen members, sitting at picnic tables, applauded while Emma and Cindy handed each of them their beds.

"That's so thoughtful and sweet," Thelma said, with several others murmuring in agreement.

"As soon as we finish our appetizers, we'll shift and head out on the hunt. Let's hurry so we can get into our thick coats before it gets dark enough for mosquitoes to come out."

The pavilion buzzed with chattering women, mostly in their sixties and seventies, with the occasional octogenarian like Josie.

At the same moment, as if spurred on by instinct rather than communication, all the club members disrobed, folding their outfits, and slipping them into tote bags.

The shifting itself, always painful and awkward, took only a couple of minutes. The pack of excited wolves, hungry for the main dishes of their picnic, jumped about like puppies. As soon as Josie took off into the forest, they loped after her.

The wolves dashed through the cypress and mahogany trees, eager to pick up a scent. But after a few miles, their pace slowed, and whining arose from the pack.

There were no raccoons, possums, or deer within sniffing distance.

Josie had warned them about what she had read: the invasive Burmese pythons that multiplied unchecked in the Everglades had decimated the population of small mammals. Josie hadn't realized it would be this bad.

She also had no way of knowing that the pythons were part of an army ordered to attack humanoids.

After the wolves returned to the picnic pavilion, dejected by the failed hunt, they shifted back to human form and got dressed. Ever the thoughtful planner, Josie had packed chicken and hamburgers in case they came up short on game. So, covered in bug spray, the women sipped wine and tried to make the best of the situation while their food sizzled on the grill.

That's when the pythons showed up.

Lisa, sitting on the end of a table at the edge of the pavilion, disappeared. Thelma, on the opposite edge, screamed and dropped out of sight.

"Thelma has a giant snake wrapped around her!" Emma screamed.

The Werewolf Women's Club erupted in panic. Half the women ran toward the minibus. The other half kicked the two snakes that had captured their friends.

Josie didn't know the reptiles had been ordered to attack humans, but she had a gut feeling the club members would be safer in wolf form.

"Ladies!" she shouted. "Shift right now. Right *now*!"

Not taking time to remove their clothes, the women shifted, tearing the garments to pieces as they went from little old ladies to muscular wolves. Sure, their coats were streaked with white hairs, but they were formidable fighters.

The python wrapped around Thelma seemed shocked to have a snarling wolf to swallow instead. Thelma sank her fangs into the snake and scratched it with her claws. The other wolves lunged at the reptile, jaws snapping. Josie seized it in her jaws just below the head and eventually pulled it from her friend.

A wolf yelped on the other side of the pavilion.

"It has Lisa!" the wolf said, which very difficult to understand thanks to her wolf's mouth mangling the words.

The wolves rushed over to find the giant snake resting on the ground with a human-sized bulge in its belly.

Despair spread throughout the pack.

Suddenly, the snake twitched and went through painful contortions.

The bulge in its body moved violently around, as if a battle was taking place in its belly.

Indeed, it was a battle. Lisa was shifting to wolf form while inside the python. The pack watched in horrified fascination while the snake's belly bubbled and rippled from limbs thrashing about inside it.

A sickening, tearing sound came.

And a wet wolf stepped from the ruptured snake she had clawed and bit her way out of.

She shook herself like a dog who just emerged from a lake, drops of snake goo flying everywhere. But no one minded. They were so happy to see Lisa emerge, like Jonah from the whale. They barked and yipped with glee, and would have wagged their tails if werewolves had tails. And at the same time, they kept a wary eye on the surrounding darkness, making sure no other reptile caught them by surprise.

The werewolves packed up the minibus while still in wolf form. It wasn't as difficult as you'd think, between their jaws and opposable thumbs, and their ability to walk upright, if needed. They packed their dog beds and picnic supplies into the bus and piled inside themselves. They waited until the bus was safely on its way to Jellyfish Beach before they shifted back to human form.

The hunt had been a disaster. The saving grace was they now had cute dog beds to curl up on.

11

VAMPIRE TOWN, USA

"You want *my* blood?" Ronnie asked incredulously. "Are you one of those crazy conspiracy theorists? I'm willing to shed my blood, but only after spilling the blood of all the vampires and humans who have wronged us."

"No, I need a *drop* of your blood," Missy said. "For a spell."

It was 3:00 a.m., and Ronnie had somehow managed to land in Missy's backyard without hitting any power lines. Though, he did knock over a palm tree by accident. He carefully avoided damaging any of her mango trees. As a young dragon rehabilitating in her garage, he had been extremely fond of mangos.

"You gave me a general idea of where your daughter, Elantha, is," Missy said. "With a drop of your blood, I can cast a spell that pinpoints her exact location. Then, we'll go in and rescue her."

She approached him with a glass vial. With his surprisingly dexterous foreleg, he pricked his shoulder with a claw. Missy held the vial beneath the wound and collected several drops before it quickly healed. Dragons had supernatural healing powers similar to those of vampires, but not as powerful. And as demonstrated by the recent deaths, dragons are not immortal.

"My dragons and I could easily rescue her once you tell me where she is."

"Ronnie, with all due respect, laying fiery waste to an entire suburban subdivision wouldn't be a good idea. Then, human law enforcement would get involved, maybe even the military. We'd have an all-out cataclysmic war on our hands."

"We are preparing for that."

"Humans have come a long way since the days of swords and arrows. I'm afraid the dragons would be wiped out. And the war would bring the supernatural to the attention of humans. It would be devastating to all the supernatural species, not just dragons."

"So be it."

"Ronnie, you've changed since I took care of you and your broken wing. You were a cute rapscallion back then."

"Now, I bear the weight of ensuring the wellbeing of my species. And my daughter has been taken from me. My rapscallion days are over."

"Give us the chance to free Elantha. We'll do a small, surgical raid. No smoldering remains of homes."

"When you cast your spell, you must tell me the location you discover. If you fail to rescue Elantha, I will do it myself."

Ronnie crouched, flapped his mighty leathery wings, and sent Missy's lawn furniture scattering across the lawn. As the wind buffeted her, he pushed off with his legs and rose above her house, flying off into the dark sky.

Missy brought the vial of blood inside to her kitchen, where she drew a large circle on her tile floor with a dry-erase marker. She lit five tea candles and placed them around the circumference, each candle at the point of an imagined pentagram, to represent the five elements. She knelt within the circle, holding the vial of blood, and began invoking the words of the locating spell.

She knew three different locating spells, but this one was the best. It used the psychic energy of the missing person, left behind on an object dear to him or her. This energy sought to reunite with its owner. In this case, the blood of the father would have ties to the blood of his daughter.

After Missy gathered power from the five elements and the reserves deep within herself, she intoned the final words.

A glowing orb appeared, floating in the air above the vial of blood.

"Find Elantha," Missy commanded.

The orb zipped across the kitchen and passed through the walls.

She sat in a meditative state and waited while the orb searched for Elantha's psychic energy.

Soon, an image came into focus in Missy's mind. An aerial view of a newer community of homes west of town. In what used to be farmland, dozens of nearly identical subdivisions had sprung up over the years as more and more people moved to Florida. Including vampires.

Residents preferred living in suburban sprawl because they wanted new homes with the latest appliances and finishes. They craved the sense of security that comes with living in a gated community, far from the older neighborhoods within the Jellyfish Beach city limits. Even some centuries-old vampires were thrilled by state-of-the-art smart fridges to hold their pints of whole blood.

The aerial image zoomed in as the orb descended and flew to the home that held the soul it sought. Soon, it hovered over a home with a barrel-tile roof. It was on a winding street with a cul-de-sac and looked like all the other homes. So, Missy directed the orb to fly lower until she could read the number on the mailbox: 16.

Next, with the image still fresh in her mind, Missy left the magic circle, ending the spell, and rushed to her laptop. She pulled up a satellite view of the Alligator Hammock community. (Ronnie had given her the general area where he sensed his daughter was. It included this community, the only one around with vampires.) She confirmed she had the right place as she found a portion of the satellite photo that resembled the image in her head. Typing in the home number, she confirmed the match: 16 Green Heron Drive.

Out of curiosity, she searched the Crab County Property Appraiser's website to learn the home was owned by Stanley Gardiner. Web searches found nothing of interest on him, but that wasn't surprising. He was most certainly a vampire if he lived in Alligator Hammock. So, his days as a live human probably ended decades, if not centuries, ago, along with his paper trail. And most vampires, Marvin being a notable exception, avoided having an online presence. Fangbook, their preferred social network, was a private intranet that was inaccessible to humans.

Now that she had an address of where Elantha was being held, Missy brought the information to Agnes.

And the rescue plan took shape.

A small team assembled. Sol and Oleg were bullied by Agnes

into accepting the mission to pay penance for previously following Bill. He wasn't even aware yet that they had decided to quit his militia, so they could fool him into trusting them. Hopefully, Stanley would allow them into his home.

Besides the two of them, the rescue team included Maria, the young vampire whom Agnes had taken under her wing, and Louis. Missy didn't know Louis, but he came armed with sharpened rebar stakes as well as firearms. The stakes, obviously, were for vampires.

"Good luck," Agnes told them. "Do not show any special treatment to the vampires. Kill them if you must. If we don't end this war, all of us vampires could die."

"Kill Bill?" Sol asked with a pang in his voice.

"Kill Bill."

A panel van, the kind that delivers packages to your neighborhood, waited by the door to the lobby. Just as the first tinges of color appeared in the sky above the ocean, the vampires piled into the storage compartment of the van. Missy got behind the wheel, and Matt sat on a jump seat on the passenger side.

"The fate of the supernatural world is in your hands," Agnes told them. "But don't be nervous."

Missy moved the van into the parking garage, deep in the shadows, where it would sit for most of the day, the vampires inside safely protected from the sun. As afternoon wore on and sunset approached, it was time to make their move.

Missy drove the van through the Jellyfish Beach gate, wondering if this was the last time they would see the building the vampires had expected to inhabit for eternity.

THE GUARD at the Alligator Hammock gatehouse didn't ask Missy which resident she was visiting. He opened the gate as soon as the van pulled up, since it was one of dozens of such trucks that had arrived during the day to deliver the vampire residents' voluminous internet purchases.

Missy still had to kill time before nightfall, so she found the community's clubhouse, an enormous facility compared to the public space at Squid Tower. She backed into the loading dock behind the building, where they could safely wait.

"What spells are you going to use?" Matt asked her.

"Mostly defensive ones. My sleep spell doesn't work on vampires, so I'll try an immobility spell I learned from a voodoo priestess, if I get the chance. But first, I'm going to place a protection spell around our vampires and the baby, Elantha, once we find her."

"What am I supposed to do?" Matt asked. "Maybe vampires can get away with killing other vampires, and humans, too, but I can't kill anyone, or I'll go to jail."

"We discussed this already." She pointed to a stack of sharpened rebar on the floor of the van. "You and I will rescue Elantha. Stake any vampire who gets in your way. You won't go to jail for that. While the others are fighting, we'll head directly for the dragon. I'll tell you where she is as soon as I sense her."

As the afternoon shadows lengthened, the two humans sat in tense silence, staring out the windows. Alligator Hammock looked like every other newish fifty-five-plus retirement community. A fountain had greeted them when they entered. Street after identical street with nearly identical homes ended in cul-de-sacs. Carefully manicured lawns. Immature palm trees. No cars parked on the street junking up the scene, as all were properly sitting in driveways or stowed in garages.

It all looked so typical except for one thing: no one was around. The place was, as they say, dead. All the undead residents were inside.

When darkness finally came, and sounds of movement and muttering drifted into the cab from the rear of the van, the neighborhood around them also came to life. So to speak.

Elderly vampire couples strutted along the streets exercising. Seniors rode by on bicycles. Two women carrying beach bags strolled past the van on their way to the swimming pool beside the clubhouse.

It was another evening in Vampire Town, USA.

The door connecting the cab to the cargo compartment slid open.

"It is time," Oleg said. "I can't stand another minute stuck back here with Louis, who smells like mothballs."

"Okay," Missy said. She started up the van, rolled slowly past a race-walking vampire, and turned onto Green Heron Drive. She parked two doors down from Number 16, a single-story home in the vaguely Mediterranean style so popular in Florida.

Bill's 1970s sedan sat in the driveway, creating a large oil stain on the concrete. Missy hoped no human militia members were in the house.

"Remember," she said to Oleg. "You and Sol are here for a social visit. Act friendly and relaxed. If you can disarm Bill and his friend, do so. If not, wait for the right moment and signal us with a whistle one of the other vampires will hear."

"Understood," Oleg said.

Missy handed him two small cloth pouches.

"What are these?"

"Amulets for you and Sol," she said. "Keep yours in your

pocket. I'm linking a protection spell to each of you, attached to the amulet."

Oleg nodded. He returned to the rear of the van. The exterior door opened, and soon he and Sol strolled along the sidewalk and turned up the front walk to Number 16. They didn't carry long arms or the rebar, to avoid alarming the neighbors, but each had concealed handguns.

It is said point-blank shots to a vampire's heart are fatal if a bullet remains lodged in the heart tissue. Bullets with wooden slugs were also available. But none of the group truly wanted to kill anyone. Unless they had to.

Missy cast the protection spell as best she could in the tight space of the cab. She could maintain only one of these bubbles of safety at a time. She built it around Oleg and Sol, attaching it to them so the bubble would enclose them wherever they went. After she created it, she sent more and more energy into it to strengthen it against projectiles. Hopefully, against bullets.

She diverted her attention to add additional magick. She created a listening spell attached to the amulets Oleg and Sol carried. It was as if they were each wearing a wire, giving Missy an audio connection as she monitored their protection spell.

Oleg and Sol went out of her view when they reached Stanley's front door. She activated the listening spell.

And hoped for the best.

12

RESCUE MISSION

In Missy's head, via the listening spell, the home's doorbell rang.

"Good evening, Mrs. Gardiner," Oleg said. "Sorry to come by so early."

"Hello Oleg, Sol," a woman with a New York accent said. "You're not too early. We've been up since sunset."

"Is Bill here?"

"Yes. He and Stanley are in the garage, oiling their guns. Come in, come in. The garage is off the kitchen. Would you like a fresh bag of Type O?"

"No thanks," Oleg said.

"I'm good," Sol added. "Love your decor."

"Thank you. I've always been a fan of mid-century funeral parlor."

"Yeah, it sure beats the beach-house look. That's so over-done in Florida."

"What's going on in there?" Matt asked Missy. He couldn't

hear the conversation since it was playing only in Missy's head.

"Vampire small talk," she said.

"It's right this way," Mrs. Gardiner said.

A door opened, the shuffling of boots.

"There you are," Bill said. "You missed drills yesterday. I was wondering about you two."

"What do you mean?" Sol asked with an edge to his voice.

"Your loyalty to the cause," Bill said.

"Exactly what cause are you following?" Oleg said. "Are you fighting the Reptilians or the dragons?"

"They're one and the same."

"No, they're not. If you want to believe in Reptilians from outer space, that's your right. I gave you the benefit of the doubt. But when you confuse the earth species of dragons with these Reptilians, that's a problem."

"You haven't done enough research," Bill said.

"You need to have your head examined, pal," Sol said. "I don't have a problem with dragons. And look, you kidnapped one of their babies. That's a serious offense."

"Are you feeding her?" Oleg asked. "She looks kind of weak."

Missy turned to Matt. "The baby's in the garage."

"I feed her hamburgers. She's fine. And if you're too spineless to support a time-honored tactic in guerrilla warfare, that's your problem."

"You're the one with a problem," Oleg said. "How old are you in body age?"

"I was sixty-nine when I was turned," Bill replied.

"That's not too young for dementia to set in."

"Knock off the personal insults," a fourth voice said. It must be Stanley's.

"You're deluded," Sol said. "Dragons are not the Reptilians.

You're dragging the vampires and humans into a war that could wipe us all out because you've got your lizards confused. I mean, why couldn't you have confused iguanas with the Reptilians? Then, we could fight an invasive species, and the earth wouldn't get destroyed."

"Marvin knew the dragons are the Reptilians," Bill said angrily.

"Marvin was deluded, too," Sol said. "You've said so yourself a million times. You told me he was a freaking nutcase."

"I was wrong," Bill said. "He was a visionary."

"Fine," Oleg said in a clipped voice. "Believe what you wish. But you must allow us to return the baby dragon."

"Never," Bill said. "If the Reptilians want their baby back, they have to surrender first and leave our planet. Though, I wouldn't trust those treacherous lizards."

"Please. Let us have the baby."

The sliding *clack* of a pistol sent a chill through Missy.

"Get out of my garage," Bill said.

"Don't point that at me," Oleg said.

"We're going in now!" Missy shouted inside the van. "Louis and Maria, go in through the front door armed with stakes. When you get to the garage, open the exterior door, and Matt and I will come in and grab the baby."

Missy hoped the two additional vampires would allow Sol and Oleg to neutralize Bill and Stanley. She hoped Stanley's wife wouldn't be a problem.

The front door busted inward as the two vampires forced their way inside. A woman screamed. With her listening spell, Missy heard the interior door to the garage open to confused shouts.

Missy glanced at Matt. "I'm worried about this."

Grunts, cursing, thuds, bangs, and body blows filled Missy's head. It was a vampire cage match.

A gun went off.

"Now, I'm really worried," Missy said.

Finally, the electric garage door slowly crawled open. Light from the garage spilled out onto the dark driveway.

"Let's go," Missy said.

She and Matt grabbed the sharpened rebar and jumped out of the van. They ran up the driveway and slipped under the half-opened door.

Inside was a chaotic scene of vampires wrestling, but the four on her team were winning. Not only did they outnumber Bill and Stanley, but they were also in better physical shape. Finally, they got the two face-down on the floor, their hand-guns safely out of reach in a far corner.

The baby dragon was in a dog crate, lying on a blanket, terrified.

"Help me carry this," Missy said to Matt.

They picked up the crate. The dragon was heavier than Missy expected. They moved the crate quickly across the garage floor and out onto the driveway.

A gun went off. Matt staggered.

Mrs. Gardiner stood in the interior doorway of the garage with a gun in her hand. She fired again. The bullet sped past Missy's ear like an angry bee.

"No!" Stanley shouted from beneath two vampires. "Don't kill the humans!"

Missy and Matt continued carrying the crate and placed it in the back of the van. That's when she saw the blood. Big droplets on the concrete driveway and the asphalt street.

And on Matt's shirt in a spreading stain. Illuminated by a streetlight, his face was as pale as a vampire's.

"Matt, you've been shot!"

He nodded.

"Let's get you to an ER now."

She helped him into the back of the van beside the crate.

"Lie down. Help me get your shirt off."

"This is hardly the time for hanky panky," Matt said in a weak voice. "But I guess I shouldn't let the opportunity slide."

Missy ignored him and pulled his T-shirt off. He had good abs, and his hairy chest was strangely appealing. But the wound on his side, just below his ribcage, grabbed her attention. She wadded the T-shirt and pressed it against the wound.

"Hold that against your side as hard as you can, no matter how much it hurts, to slow the bleeding."

She rushed to the van's cab.

"Hey, are you guys coming?" She shouted to her vampire team. She didn't want to leave them behind. "I have to take Matt to the hospital."

Tires screeched as two pickups and a Jeep pulled up in front of Stanley's home. Six human militia members jumped out and immediately opened fire on Stanley's house.

Missy ducked beneath the dashboard but managed to peek out at what was going on.

The militia men were ready for a fight. But they clearly weren't sure who they were fighting. They sprayed the front of Stanley's home with gunfire, perforated Bill's parked car, and then shot at other homes in the neighborhood.

"Yee-haw!" one of them yelled.

They appeared to be firing at everything. Except their own

vehicles. And, for some reason, they spared the delivery van where Missy and Matt were hiding.

The militants kept firing, spent cartridges raining upon the street, empty magazines dropping randomly. The men were in an almost orgiastic glee. Shooting was an end in itself, regardless of what they hit. They were entranced in gunpowder ecstasy.

Missy called 911 and reported the gunfire. Hopefully, these yahoos would end up in jail.

The vampires in the garage remained lying on the floor in their wrestling holds. Bill must be itching to shoot so badly, Missy thought. But the vampires had to stay down to avoid being hit.

Stanley suddenly broke free from Louis and Maria. He grabbed a handgun from the floor. Louis crouched with a rebar, ready to plunge it into Stanley.

But instead of shooting at the vampires in his garage, Stanley fired at the militia, his own comrades in arms.

After all, they were shooting his home to pieces. They weren't his comrades anymore.

Of course, his gunshots only encouraged the assailants in the street. Their rate of fire increased. And they directed it into the garage.

Someone pressed the button to lower the garage door, but it was too late. Stanley staggered backwards, hit multiple times. His wife screamed.

Missy didn't know if the bullets would be lethal for the vampire but wouldn't be surprised if they were.

She crawled into the cargo area to check on Matt. He was conscious and gritted his teeth in pain. The T-shirt against his wound was fully soaked in blood, but it seemed to be doing its job at slowing the bleeding.

She cast a quick spell to further slow the bleeding. It wasn't enough, but it was the only magick she knew for this situation.

Sirens blared not far away.

"Finally, the police are coming," she said. "An ambulance will take you to the hospital."

She glanced at the dragon in her crate. The poor creature was terrorized.

"I can't let the police find the dragon, but I can't drive away until they get here and stop the shooting. But then they probably won't allow me to leave without being questioned."

"Sucks to be you," Matt said.

The militia men, who just shot one of their own members, low-crawled toward the garage. Finally, they had someone to shoot at, and they weren't about to give up this opportunity.

The garage door was taking its sweet time lowering while being peppered with bullets.

Finally, the motor took a round, and the door stopped, halfway closed.

And now, all the vampires in the garage were shooting at the humans.

The air was practically dripping with cordite, adrenaline, and testosterone.

One of the militants, a big guy with a beard, went down. This only caused his comrades to fire more enthusiastically.

Strobe lights hit them as several police cars arrived.

"Put down your weapons," a male officer said through the loudspeaker. "Police. Put down your weapons!"

The militia ignored them.

Not to be left out from the gunfire extravaganza, the police officers, taking cover behind their opened car doors, began firing, too.

"Oh, my," Missy said. "This is getting plain stupid."

The Alligator Hammock retirement community was now experiencing more gunfire than many World War II battles.

The police fired at the militia and the vampires, the militia fired at the vampires, and the vampires fired at the militia. Trapped in the crossfire, half the militia got the not very bright idea to return fire at the police.

The intensity of the gun battle increased, if that was even possible at this point.

Two more militia members went down, leaving only three still fighting. They finally snapped out of their firing frenzy and dropped their weapons.

The shooting petered out, like the final detonations of microwave popcorn.

At last, Missy thought. The humans would be arrested, and the police would investigate their ties to the militia. She hoped that would drive them into hiding.

She worried about the vampires. Vampires don't do well in jail. She suspected Bill was the only one who fired directly at the police. He could go to jail for all she cared, as long as the ones on her team talked their ways out of this.

The scene appeared to be secure as the police officers fanned through the battleground.

That's when the dragons arrived.

A troop of four flew overhead, with the absolutely worst timing. Ronnie must have probed Missy's thoughts and discovered what was going on and where his baby was. They were coming for her rescue.

Bad idea, dragons.

The dragons swooped in. The humans on the ground stared upward at them in amazement.

"Reptilians!" a disarmed militia member shouted.

Before he went up in flames.

The dragons torched all the militia members, one by one, as they glided slowly over the scene. The police ran to their cars for cover. The giant beasts had the good sense not to attack the police.

But the damage had already been done. The dragons had revealed themselves to humans and, worst of all, the police. This would escalate the human-reptile conflict into truly cataclysmic levels.

Missy sat in the cab, not sure of what to do. Should she try to drive away now that the police were distracted?

Her question was answered when the van jolted to the side, and she almost fell out of the seat. She watched the ground drop away as the van was lifted into the air.

The neighborhood battlefield grew smaller as the van, with her, Matt, and the baby dragon inside, was carried off into the night by the dragons.

THE FLIGHT WAS SURPRISINGLY SMOOTH. But Missy couldn't say it was relaxing. Flying in a commercial jetliner is one thing. Flying in a package-delivery van meant to have all four tires always touching the road, was terrifying.

Plus, she had a patient in the back with a bullet wound who should be in the ER right now, not 20,000 feet above Florida.

"Are we on the way to the hospital?" Matt asked.

Missy realized Matt, lying on his back on the floor of the

van, didn't know they'd been picked up by dragons as if they were prey to be eaten.

"We're taking a little detour," she said. "But don't worry. You'll be fine."

"That's what my accountant said to me at tax time. Turned out he was wrong."

A single-engine plane flew by the left side of the truck, only slightly faster than they were going. It was so close Missy could see the pilot stare at them with his mouth open. She wondered what was strangest to him, to see the dragons or the flying delivery truck?

She waved. The pilot belatedly waved back.

The dragons really messed up today if they wanted to keep their existence secret from humans.

A horrifying thought hit her. What if the pilot reported them and a squadron of fighter jets came and intercepted them? Dragons carrying a delivery van wouldn't stand a chance. The occupants of the van wouldn't either.

Her stomach lurched as the van dropped in altitude. But the queasy feeling remained, along with a vertiginous anxiety.

She recognized the feeling. It was how she felt before she entered a gateway to the In Between, the alternate plane of existence between worlds. Dragons used the In Between as a haven from humans once the earth became overpopulated with us. She'd been here before for short periods of time.

She worried how it would affect Matt in his condition.

Suddenly, the sky outside the windshield shimmered like a curtain of water. Her vision went black for a few seconds. When she regained her sight, she gasped.

THE VAN SAT atop a rocky plateau in a landscape that looked like Arizona. Except it was as far from the Grand Canyon State as you could get. The sky was the featureless white that Missy remembered from before.

She went into the back to check on Matt.

"Something strange happened," he said. "Where the heck are we?"

"Do you remember me mentioning the In Between before?"

"You've got to be kidding me! We're there?"

Missy nodded.

"Um, why?"

"The dragons took us here."

"You mean picked us up and carried us here from Alligator Hammock?"

"Yeah. In front of the cops and other witnesses. I didn't say anything because I didn't want you to panic while we were flying through the sky. We're safe now. Temporarily."

The dragons who had captured them alighted on nearby outcroppings. Ronnie's voice appeared in Missy's head.

Is my daughter safe? I know she's in your van.

Yes. I'll put her outside.

Missy carefully opened the rear doors. The plateau where they'd been placed wasn't much bigger than the van, but there was room for the dragon. Knowing they wouldn't be happy seeing her in the dog crate, she opened its door.

"Are you okay, little one? Would you like to see your parents?"

Elantha was no longer terrified. She knew her parents were outside. Missy reached into the crate to handle her. A small jet of flame made her jerk her hands out.

"Okay, I see you've had enough of humanoids. You can get out on your own."

The dragon waddled out of the crate onto the floor of the van. She continued to the open door and looked out, eyes blinking.

"You need help getting down to the ground?"

The dragon showed her razor teeth and hissed.

Missy raised her hands. "Just asking."

The dragon flapped her wings and jumped from the van. She landed softly on the rock floor, but you couldn't call what she did flying.

Elantha was smaller and obviously younger than Ronnie had been when Missy saved him and nursed him while his broken wing healed. She was amazed at how fast Ronnie had grown up and become a father. It was especially striking when you consider dragons live for hundreds of years.

Dust kicked up from the rocky ground and Missy was buffeted by wind from the wings of approaching dragons. From behind the van, Ronnie appeared, flying close. He fixed Missy with one eye.

Thank you, he said.

Hovering in mid-air, he opened his giant, deadly mouth, lined with sharp teeth and hardened cartilage that could withstand jets of flame. And with that formidable weapon, he gingerly grasped his child and flew away. The van rocked from the force of the displaced air.

Missy waved goodbye.

Wait, she thought. What are we going to do now? We're trapped atop a rock fifty feet in the air. And we need to find a gateway to get back home.

Another dragon appeared, a female. She was about to land

on the rock, so Missy stepped to the side of the van to make room.

I am Ursula, the Healer. You have a wounded human in need of care?

Yes. He's in the van. He was wounded by a gunshot. I'm pretty sure the bullet exited, and I don't believe it hit a vital organ.

The dragon, greener in color than Ronnie, shuffled to the van and poked her head inside.

Matt squealed in fear.

"It's okay," Missy said. "She's a healer."

"But she's a dragon and dragons don't like me."

"It was Ronnie who didn't like you when I was taking care of him. It was only male jealousy."

"That's all it was. Now I—"

His voice cut out at the same time Missy felt the magic pouring from the dragon. Benevolent, pure healing magic. If only Missy's magick could be as strong as that for healing, she could do much good for her supernatural patients and for humans, too.

The dragon stuck her long neck far into the van, touching Matt's wounded side. Missy couldn't tell what was going on, but the healing magic flowed and intensified.

About ten minutes later, the dragon backed away from the van and looked directly at Missy.

He should be fine now. Get him what you humans call antibiotics. Or the magical equivalent.

Thank you so much, Missy said as the healer soared away over the canyon.

13

A BIG DISASTER

Matt wouldn't stop staring at his side where the bullet wound had disappeared, leaving no trace save for dried blood. He poked at his skin.

"It's like it never happened," he said.

"That is some powerful healing. Someday, I'd like my magick to do that."

"If you had put a protection spell on us, it wouldn't have happened."

Missy felt a pang of regret. "I had no choice but to put it on Oleg and Sol. They were going into the most dangerous situation. Unfortunately, I don't have enough power to maintain more than one protection bubble strong enough to stop a bullet."

"It's okay. Bill and Stanley had been disarmed. Who would have known the wife was packing heat?"

"I wish I had a spell to smack her around a bit for shooting you."

"What do you think happened to the vampires? You say the cops showed up?"

"They sure did," Missy said. "And Bill was shooting at them."

"Uh-oh."

"And the police saw the dragons."

"Uh-oh."

"This has escalated into a big disaster. Now that Ronnie has his daughter back, he should declare a truce."

"And cancel whatever spell he used to make all the reptiles go nuts. A gopher tortoise broke into my bungalow and dug a burrow in my bed. And I won't go into detail about the snake in the bathtub."

Missy shuddered.

"We can't stay here in the In Between. But I'm kind of dreading going back to earth with all the problems festering there."

"I don't care about them. I just want to go back. How do we get home?"

"We need to find a gateway. They're constantly moving and could appear anywhere. Unfortunately, we're stuck on this plateau."

"We'll climb down."

"It's a sheer cliff face. And we're Floridians. We don't know how to climb rocks. We don't even know how to climb hills."

"I don't care. I'll . . . what's that?"

"It's a gateway!" Missy said.

A vertical disc of shimmering air had entered the van's cargo hold between Missy and Matt.

And then Matt was gone. The gateway had floated quickly toward Matt and engulfed him. Missy rushed toward the portal so she, too, could pass through. But the gateway zipped out of the rear doors. It floated past the edge of the plateau, fifty feet in the air, as if daring Missy to risk leaping after it.

It faded away.

Great, she thought. Now I'm stranded here alone. With no food or water. And the rental van needs to be returned.

IN THE DARK OF NIGHT, Matt landed softly on a lawn of thick grass. Unfortunately, the sprinkler system was running, soaking him. He scrambled to his feet and escaped into the street.

That's when he noticed the homeowners staring at him. They stood outside their front door and looked at him as if he were a two-headed cow. Having someone materialize out of thin air onto your carefully manicured lawn has that effect.

The elderly couple had ghastly white skin and pointy ears. Vampires. Matt glanced around at the surrounding homes and realized he had returned to Alligator Hammock. Ahead, where the street went around a bend, flashing lights painted the asphalt.

He waved to the vampires and trudged toward the crime scene to scope out what was going on. His reporter instincts were stronger than his common sense which told him to get the heck out of the neighborhood.

There were dozens of police cars, several ambulances, two firetrucks, and an armored SWAT vehicle—all with strobe lights flashing. Matt hadn't seen the SWAT vehicle before in all his reporting on crime in the city. Jellyfish Beach was where murders were exceptionally rare, and the majority of police incidents involved complaints about someone else's dog pooping on your lawn.

Uh-oh, he thought. Channel Six already had a reporter here. As he drew closer, he heard her making a live report. "Attacked by an armed militia," caught his ears.

The street was covered in spent cartridges, as if they had fallen in a metal hailstorm. Streetlights had been shot out, mailboxes torn to shreds, and windows of the houses nearest Stanley's all had shattered windows.

Don't these guys know how to aim? he wondered.

Crime scene investigators climbed in and out of the two pickups and the Jeep belonging to the militants. The vehicles, of course, were riddled with bullet holes.

As he moved to a position to better see the Gardiner's home, he froze.

Six bodies covered in tarps lay on the street in front of Stanley's home. Matt's heart rate went up.

The light was still on in Stanley's garage, and the door remained frozen halfway open. Inside, numerous pairs of legs could be seen moving about, many of them in police uniforms.

A police officer guarded the front door. She moved aside, and one by one, officers led seven vampires outside in handcuffs. The Gardiners and Bill, followed by Sol, Oleg, Louis, and Maria.

None had been shot to death or staked. Stanley appeared to have recovered from the bullet wounds. Matt didn't care much for the vampires, but he knew Missy was fond of them.

The vampires had the strength and speed, even in their elderly bodies, to escape from the police before they were handcuffed. But they weren't stupid. They knew their survival depended on keeping their vampirism secret.

The question was, could they keep it secret while being interrogated and possibly thrown into the county jail?

Matt could keep a secret. He still had his notebook and pen in his pocket, and he used them to get quotes from the neighbors about what they had seen tonight. He would write a story about the shootout and submit it before the rapidly approaching deadline.

And he wouldn't mention that all the neighbors he interviewed were vampires.

IT SEEMED like hours had passed until the van rocked on its suspension as it was hit by wind. A dragon flew in and landed on the rock behind it. The dragon was Ronnie. His words filled Missy's head.

You must be wondering why you weren't sent home.

Yes. My thoughts, exactly.

I will always be grateful for what you did for me in the past and for helping rescue my daughter, he said. *But I am king now, and I must make difficult decisions that sometimes go against my heart.*

What are you saying?

The elder dragon lords have demanded that we keep you as a hostage. You are the vampires' healer, and they won't get you back until they give us the ones who started all of this. The vampire named Marvin, and the one named Bill.

Marvin is dead. Didn't you guys kill him?

No, we did not.

Bill, you can have on a silver platter, as far as I'm concerned. He's gone too far. In fact, if you let me go home, I'll bring him to you.

Ronnie chuckled.

You're still the same Missy I knew. I apologize for this. The dragons haven't had a king for centuries, and the old dragon lords resent me for being the Anointed One and usurping their dominance. I'm trying to show them I respect their wisdom. But if they keep issuing ultimatums, I'll have to come down hard on their behinds. Our dragons can't afford a destabilizing rebellion against me. In the meantime, I'll make sure you are comfortable here and protected from harm.

That's not very reassuring, Missy thought to herself as the giant dragon took flight, leaving the van rocking.

"Detective Affird, how can I assist you?" Agnes asked after she opened her door to find the tall, thin cop who always wore shades.

"I came by here today, but no one answered their doors," Affird said with a knowing smirk.

"You didn't ring my doorbell. I was home all day."

"I didn't want to trouble you, but I'm afraid I must now. Five residents of Squid Tower are at the station being interviewed after they were involved in a shootout with a militia in Alligator Hammock."

"Oh gods,"

"*Gods?* Plural?"

"You misunderstood. I said God, singular." A Visigoth noble-woman, Agnes had not yet been converted to Christianity when she was turned in 571 A.D. After all these centuries, she still slipped up sometimes and evoked the pagan gods.

"One resident is a young woman who gave your condo as her address."

"That must be Maria. She's a friend of my granddaughter and is staying with me for a while. Is she all right?"

Agnes' granddaughter actually died in 620 A.D., but Affird would never know that.

"None of your neighbors were injured. Even though our police sharpshooter swears he put a few rounds into one man."

"That is good to know. Are they in trouble with the law?"

"Only one of them fired at the police. He's in trouble. But others admitted they brought weapons to the home where the shooting took place, allegedly for self-protection relating to a dispute."

"Which one of our residents fired at the police?"

"I can't release his name right now. But I will say he is a member of the militia that showed up and shot at the home."

"Ah, Bill Meany. He still owns his condo here, but he's no longer a resident. We kicked him out for breaking the bylaws and other offenses."

"Okay. That's why he appeared to be staying at the home that was attacked."

"How else can I help you, Detective?" Agnes asked in a tone indicating she wanted this interaction to end.

Affird pulled the door open a little wider.

"Allow me to lay my cards on the table. I suspect your community is full of vampires. I've suspected it for a very long time. You've known I've suspected it. But I've never had enough proof to do anything about it. And many others in the department would laugh at me if I accused you. Technically, it's not illegal to be a vampire, unless you assault people. But last night pushed me to the breaking point."

"Why is that, Detective?"

"The dragons."

"Dragons?"

"Yes. Like the kind in fantasy movies. They attacked the

militia members and carried away a delivery van. We saw it happen. Though my colleagues are in denial mode right now."

"Why would I know anything about dragons?" Agnes asked, trying her best to look ignorant.

"Because they're supernatural, like vampires."

"Dragons are more lizard than supernatural."

"Whatever." Affird was getting frustrated. "Vampires were under attack, and dragons showed up to rescue them."

"What makes you believe they showed up to rescue them? The dragons may have had another motive. After all, they took away a delivery van. Didn't you say so yourself?"

"Why would dragons want a delivery van?"

"The package they were expecting was late?"

"It was a rental van. And it just so happens we checked with the rental company. They said the van hadn't been returned and was missing. And you know who rented it?"

"A dragon?"

Affird's face turned beet-red.

"Bill Meany?" Agnes guessed.

"No," Affird said. "Missy Mindle. The home health nurse who comes here every night and pretends she doesn't believe in vampires."

"Oh. Well, I haven't the foggiest idea why Missy rented the van, and why it was there last night."

"I believe you do know. That is why I'm here tonight. May I come in and ask you more questions?"

"I supposed you may. Do I need a lawyer?"

"You do not. But I can't prevent you from calling one. I'd rather just get this over with and allow you to enjoy your evening."

Agnes invited Affird into her living room and offered him a

bottled water, which he declined. She considered whether she should mesmerize the detective and make him forget why he came here, or about all the vampire stuff. She worried he would later be reminded by his case notes. His blacked-out evening would make him even more suspicious. She held off on mesmerizing him. For now.

He peppered her with questions about Bill and the four other Squid Tower residents who had been detained. What where they doing at the house? Why were they armed? Were drugs involved? Was anyone else other than Bill involved with the militia?

She claimed to be unable to answer any of the questions, except to assert that Bill was the only one with militia ties.

"Don't stonewall me, Ms. Geberich."

"I am offended you accuse me of that."

"Please help me out here. I don't want to take serious measures."

"Serious measures? What do you mean?"

"I will be in your face every day. Make that every night. I will watch your community like a hawk. You're not making a fool out of me anymore. I'm going to get proof that you're all vampires, somehow in league with the dragons, and I'm going to shut you down."

"Do you realize what you just said?" Agnes asked. "Wouldn't your supervisor send you to get counseling after making such outlandish accusations? Are you one of those internet conspiracy nuts?"

Affird's face tightened, and he sat upright on the couch.

"No, not the internet. Vampires have been part of folklore for as long as humans have existed. I refuse to ignore you any longer. You live in my community and make it dangerous to the families who live here."

"Detective, please. When was the last time you had an assault victim with signs of being bitten by a vampire?"

"It's time to take me seriously, Ms. Geberich. I've staked a vampire before. And I've killed werewolves. I refuse to allow you supernatural freaks to endanger my community anymore. I'm going to shut you down. If that means locking you all up, or staking all of you, so be it."

He stood, his body rigid with anger, and ready to fight.

Agnes could snap his head off his pencil neck in an instant, and drink the fountain of his blood, if she wanted to. The only reason this little jerk was alive was the importance of keeping the vampires' existence absolutely secret.

Affird had always posed a threat to them. Now, it was at crisis level.

But he didn't realize who he was picking a fight with.

14

RONNIE, DRAGON KING

Agnes' buzzer rang again.

"Ye gods, who could this be now?" Oops, she needed to be careful about the plural gods thing.

When she answered, she was surprised to see a tall young man standing there. He was dressed all in white, with his silk shirt unbuttoned enough to reveal well-defined pectoral muscles, as if he mistook this for a paranormal romance story. It was rare to see anyone under sixty in body age at Squid Tower, except for delivery people. The landscapers and contractors showed up only during the day when the vampires slept.

So, who was this handsome fellow with spiky brown hair and eyes a luminescent shade of green?

"Mrs. Geberich, good evening."

"You seem familiar. Do I know you?"

"Yes, but you've only met me in dragon form. I'm Ronnie, King of the Dragons."

"Oh, pleasure to see you again. I didn't know until recently that dragons can shape-shift."

"Very few of us can. I gained the ability when I reached adulthood. I'm from a line of dragons called the Anointed Ones. It's why I was crowned as our king. Although, some of my rivals from older generations don't necessarily agree with that."

"Please come in. Would you like water? Or do dragons prefer something else? I'm fresh out of maiden blood."

"No, thank you. I can't stay long. I've come to speak with you about Missy."

"Do you know where she is? We haven't seen or heard from her."

"She's in good health, but she's being held in the In Between. Are you aware of this place?"

"I've only heard of it," Agnes said.

"The senior dragon lords who form my council have demanded we detain Missy until she is exchanged for the vampires who started the hostilities between humanoids and dragons. I am told one is named Marvin, and the other, more violent one, is called Bill. The one who attacked us during our parley. When those individuals are delivered to us, we will call a truce. We will cease all hostilities, and I will break the spell causing the reptiles and amphibians of earth to rise up."

"Oh," Agnes said. "Peace would be lovely, but your request is complicated."

"During our parley, you said you wouldn't hand over your vampires to us to face justice. I understand that. But the dragon lords refuse to release Missy without receiving the criminal vampires in return."

"Well, I may have changed my mind."

"That is good to hear."

"But, as I said, there are complications. First, Marvin Nutley is dead. Some believe dragons incinerated him."

"Right. And we didn't do it."

"And the other main culprit, Bill Meany, is in police custody now. If and when he gets released, we'll see what we can do."

"I understand it's difficult to hand over one of your own."

"No. With Bill, it wouldn't be difficult anymore. What will you do to him? Eat him?"

"He will be imprisoned, and we will hold a trial. After he is judged, a punishment will be determined."

"How do we get him to you? And how do we get Missy back?"

"Dragons are telepathic. Concentrate on my name and speak to me with your mind. Keep trying until I answer. Then I will arrange for the transfer."

"Okay. One other thing, do you realize the police saw your dragons last night?"

Ronnie hung his head.

"That wasn't the best idea," he said. "But I had to rescue my daughter whom Bill had kidnapped. It turned out that Missy had her, but I sensed she was in danger when the crazy human militia attacked. I was too impulsive, but it couldn't be helped."

"We need to do something about this. If word spreads among the humans that dragons exist, we won't be able to end the war. And the vampires' secret existence is at risk, as well."

"We dragons have magic that can make humans forget."

"You'd better dump a huge load of it all over Jellyfish Beach before it's too late."

"As soon as the hostilities end. I need to go now. Thank you for meeting with me. Let me know when we can make the transfer."

The handsome young man left. He reminded Agnes of a particularly attractive Visigoth warrior she knew in her youth, but the dragon was much better groomed and didn't smell.

She picked up her phone and called each member of the Squid Tower HOA Board of Directors.

"THIS EMERGENCY BOARD meeting is now in session," Agnes said with a rap of the piece of wood she used as a gavel. It was part of a stake that had executed a violator of the bylaws years ago and represented the board's absolute authority over the vampires.

It was fitting, as tonight they discussed the fate of one of their own.

"You honestly think I would object to giving that lunatic to the dragons?" Schwartz asked.

"No, not you," Gloria said. "You would sell your own mother to them."

"I don't know if this is right," Kim said. "It feels like a betrayal. I didn't mind sending vampires to fight him for the dragon baby, but to give him up to other creatures? I don't know. And Bill's a board member, and he's not here to defend himself."

"We know what kinds of cockamamie conspiracies he'd spout off to defend himself," Schwartz said.

"He started a war," Gloria said.

"Marvin started it," Kim said.

"Marvin began the violence, but Bill escalated it needlessly into a war," Agnes said. "A war that threatens all vampires and the entire planet."

"Worse, there was an iguana in my toilet," Gloria said.

"I've lost track of how many vampires have been harmed because of that knucklehead," Schwartz said.

"Because of the dragons. They torched four vampires on the golf course. And Marvin."

"They didn't torch Marvin," Agnes said. "I believe Bill may have been the one who locked him on his balcony."

"Another reason to give him to the dragons," Schwartz said.

"We used to be friends with Bill," Kim said in a quiet voice.

"Used to be is the key." Gloria said. "Bill is no longer Bill. He's nuts. He went off the deep end. His mind has been poisoned by his ridiculous conspiracy theories. I can't be sympathetic to someone who dragged himself into the abyss. It's a tragedy of his own making."

"Allow me to remind you all," Agnes said, leaning forward and placing her hands on the table. "Our bylaws include rules meant to protect our community from being revealed to the world and destroyed. If a vampire kills prey, or even hunts too close to the community, he or she can be banished."

"Bill was already banished," Kim said.

"If a vampire harms another vampire, he can be staked. Bill has harmed us all, both indirectly and directly."

The board members mumbled in affirmation.

"I move we bring the issue to a vote," Agnes said.

"Seconded," said Schwartz.

"All in favor of handing Bill to the dragons say 'aye.'"

Four "ayes." Kim had been persuaded.

"The motion has passed," Agnes said.

"How are we going to hand him over?" Schwartz asked.

"I'll call our attorney, Paul Leclerc. Assuming the judge sets bail, we'll bail him out. Then we capture him when he leaves jail."

"How much are we willing to put up for bail?" Schwartz asked. "You do realize we'll lose it all if Bill goes to the dragons and doesn't appear for his trial."

"We'll pay whatever price we must for peace," Agnes said.

"And to an end to all this nonsense about Reptilians," Kim said.

"Great," Schwartz muttered. "We'll all get charged a special assessment to pay for his bail. Just great."

BILL KNEW he was in deep doo-doo.

It was one thing to strut around with weapons and talk about taking down the government when you had no intention of doing anything. Even firing your weapons in public, at a golf course, seemed acceptable when you were shooting at Reptilians from another planet.

But shooting at cops? Lots of guys in the militia talked about doing it and never had or would. But he did. Police don't take kindly to being shot at, even if you're the greatest patriot ever.

The detective who loved to prowl around Squid Tower—the one who wore shades at night—sat across a conference room table from Bill. He didn't say anything, only stared with his eyes inscrutable behind the dark lenses.

Bill had been shot near the end of the battle, but his wound had healed supernaturally. The bullet hadn't gone into his heart. His body still ached, though. And it was early morning, past dawn. The room was windowless, yet Bill felt queasy.

Bill had called the lawyer the board used, the werewolf

named Leclerc. But the bum refused to represent Bill, said he had a conflict. Did that mean the Board was using Leclerc against him?

Bill requested a public defender instead. The attorney wouldn't know Bill was a vampire, and he or she probably didn't work nighttime hours. Bill's survival depended upon being in only windowless rooms during the day. When they sent him to the county jail, could he avoid sunlight there?

Yeah, Bill was in deep doo-doo.

Not even counting what the guys of ERR were thinking. Bill had ordered them to come to Stanley's house to turn the tide against the weasels from Squid Tower. And look how that turned out.

All six of them were dead, shot by police or torched by Reptilians. But the rest of the guys at ERR wouldn't know about the flying lizards. They would think the police killed all six men. Would they blame Bill for summoning them to the house?

"What kind of mood are you in?" Affird asked out of the blue.

"What do you mean? I'm under arrest. What kind of mood do you think I'm in?"

"I mean, are you in the mood to make a deal?"

Bill paused. "Depends."

Affird leaned back and put his feet on the table.

"I don't need to make any deals. I've got you nailed seven ways to Sunday. But deals are the oil that makes the justice system work faster."

"Are you talking about a plea deal?" Bill asked.

"Eventually. That will be between you, your lawyer, and the prosecutor. I'm talking about a deal between you and me, to move this process along. To make it easier for both of us."

"Go on."

"Mr. Meany, I know you're a vampire. I could stake you right here and now."

Bill gulped.

"You won't last more than a day or two in the county jail. As soon as someone figures you out, you're a goner. A correctional officer or an inmate, one of them's going to stake you. And get away with it."

Bill sat silently, clenching his teeth, his fangs safely retracted.

"You being a vampire doesn't concern me so much right now," Affird went on. "I know Squid Tower is full of bloodsuckers like you. I'm planning to shut the whole place down and send all your neighbors to Hell where they belong. Whether you're with them or not. What I'm most concerned about now is this armed militia you seem to be in command of. I don't want armed lunatics running around in Jellyfish Beach, shooting up neighborhoods."

"You want me to turn on them?" Bill asked.

"That's not the way I would have put it, but yes. Give me everything you've got on them. I want to put the bad ones away and send the others scurrying into cracks like roaches."

"Do I need to wear a wire?"

"Possibly. I don't know yet. For now, you can tell me everything about them. Give me names and numbers. Let me know what kind of hardware they've amassed. All your planned operations. Etcetera. I'll have the D.A. request an immediate bond hearing, with a low amount. We'll get you out of jail before you even get hungry for blood. Then, we'll work on that plea deal. Are you interested?"

"Yes." Bill didn't even hesitate.

Affird removed a notebook from his pocket.

"Remember," he said, "this conversation is being recorded. Begin wherever you want."

"Reptilians," Bill said. "It began with the Reptilians."

"You mean the dragons?"

"They're not dragons. They're Reptilians. They can shift into any shape they want, though. Usually, they look like humans so they can blend into society and take it over."

"You're a conspiracy buff?"

"The truth is not a conspiracy. The truth is a reward to those who dig deep enough to find it."

"Maybe I made a mistake with this deal," Affird said.

"My organization, Earthlings Resisting Reptilians, is fighting to save the human race."

"Does that mean you're not going to give me the information I need?" Affird asked.

"No, I'll tell you everything you want to know, as long as you don't make me stay in jail. Okay, my battlefield commander is Abe Washington. Former military. Spent some time behind bars for possession of a surface-to-air missile."

Bill continued talking for hours.

ON HIS SECOND, horrible night in the county jail. Bill received a visitor. He wasn't told who it was, so he was shocked to see Paul Leclerc sitting on the other side of the plexiglass.

"Paul! What are you doing here? I thought you wouldn't represent me."

"I'm representing the Board, and we're bailing you out," said the shaggy, older attorney who wore a ponytail despite being bald on top. "The Board raised the money, and you're out of here, as soon as the jail can do the paperwork."

"For real?"

"For real. I'm going to wait in the visitors' lot and give you a ride home. To wherever you're staying, that is. You're still banned from Squid Tower."

Bill wanted to curse out the prissy little jerks who banned him but held his tongue.

"That's great," he said. "Thank you."

Two hours later, he was back in civilian clothes, holding a manilla envelope with the personal items taken from his pockets. He walked out into the humid night air and took a deep, grateful breath. This wasn't the end of his legal battle, but if the plea deal worked out, he wouldn't have to see the jail ever again.

He looked around for Leclerc's car, not knowing what the lawyer drove. Finally, a BMW pulled up.

Leclerc was driving. But in the backseat were Oleg and Louis. Two of the vampires who had attacked him at Stanley's house. What were they doing in the car?

Bill hesitated. He had a bad feeling about this.

An SUV approached from the back of the parking lot and cut off the BMW. The tinted window rolled down to reveal Abe.

"Abe! What are you doing here?" Bill asked in his friendliest voice.

"Stopping you from ratting out the militia," Abe said, pulling a grenade launcher into view.

IT IS SAID that North Korea's Kim Jong-un once ordered an anti-aircraft gun to be used to execute officials who angered him. Aiming a grenade launcher at an individual at close range was in the same spirit.

It's impossible to say if Abe knew Bill was a vampire. But his choice of such an over-the-top weapon ensured that even a vampire wouldn't survive the grenade impact plus the explosion.

The three men in the BMW were lucky to survive, though they sat stunned among the smoke and shattered glass, while the SUV sped away.

Bill was out of their hair forever. But now they didn't have anyone to trade to get Missy back.

15

KNOCK-DOWN-DRAGON FIGHT

Missy could tell the water and food the dragons gave her weren't real. They were created from magic, since there is no actual sustenance available in the In Between. The water and food were convincing, though. They slaked her thirst and filled her belly. But the food had a little too much sodium. If you're ever in the In Between, don't order the dragon version of Swedish Meatballs.

The roll of toilet paper she requested was also not real. The good part is it meant the portions she used disappeared into thin air moments after she was finished with them.

Spending her days on a flat rock five stories tall and sleeping in the van were taking a toll on her. There was no conception of day or night here. The dull white light of the sky never waxed or waned. Her watch and phone did not work here, so she never knew what time it was. She passed the hours by sleeping when she was tired and practicing magick spells. Magick was a challenge here, since she normally drew energy from the five elements of earth, or from ley lines, along with the energies within her own body. Here, in the In Between, there was no energy she could harvest. All she had was what was in her, amplified by the power charm she always carried. That, at least, still worked here.

One day (or was it night?), a dragon approached from far away on the opposite side of the vast canyon. Since Missy first arrived, she hadn't seen any dragons except for Ronnie.

This was not Ronnie. The dragon was slightly larger than him, with a darker brownish-gray coloring. As it neared her, she saw moss and other signs of old age on its scales. Its eyes were glowing green and hostile.

It circled her plateau and landed near the van in a cloud of dust.

You are the human witch? the dragon asked in a male voice inside her head.

Yes. I'm Missy Mindle.

I am Lord Rembert. I came to see what, if anything, you are worth.

Don't judge me by my salary. I'm terribly underpaid.

Is your magic as strong as ours?

Um, not really. But I probably know some spells you guys don't.

We do not need spells to create magic, Rembert said. *We simply use the magic we were born with.*

Why are you asking?

I'm judging if you are worth keeping alive.

Missy's heart skipped a beat. *I thought I would be part of a prisoner exchange.*

The human we wanted to bring to justice is now dead, killed by one of the killers who followed him.

Oh, my.

The other lords of the council question if we should kill you.

Tell them the answer is "no."

We wish to make you an example of what happens when humans attack us without provocation.

Missy was panicking now. *But I didn't harm any dragon. Remember, I'm the one who helped heal King Ronnie when he was young.*

Young and weak, as he remains to this day.

Ronnie, help! she called in her mind.

Your friend, the king, should have responded with more force when the humans attacked us.

Vampires, not humans, Missy thought. And then regretted it when Rambert extended his neck toward her and bared his teeth.

The missile streaked across the pale sky in a brown-green blur.

It was Ronnie. He slammed into Rembert like a freight train. The sound of the collision echoed throughout the canyon. Missy scampered into the van for safety.

The two dragons plunged from view down the side of the plateau. They reappeared on the other side, Ronnie in pursuit of Rembert as he flew at a sharp angle high into the atmosphere.

Ronnie caught up to Rembert and seized him with his talons. Rembert turned, and they wrestled stomach to stomach, raking each other with sharp talons, beating each other with their wings, whipping the tails with tips like spear points.

Drops of blood rained down past the van's windows.

Rembert broke free and dove into the canyon.

How dare you attack me! Missy heard Rembert say in her head.

I am your king, and I've had enough of your disrespect.

You haven't earned the right to be my king. I am wiser and more powerful than you.

Ronnie let out a screeching roar and caught his rival once again. They smashed against the side of the plateau, and the van rocked with the vibrations.

Missy wanted to help her friend. She didn't use attack spells, but she could try to place a protection bubble around Ronnie. With no energies to draw from the environment, she dug deep within herself inside a hastily drawn magick circle in the back of the van.

It was difficult to concentrate with the battle going on above and below.

Mid-spell, something caught her eye. Another dragon approached. It was larger and darker, like Rembert. Was it one of his allies? She desperately worked on her spell, weaving strands of magick and purpose, adding power from her own heart and soul amplified by the power charm.

You will not hurt King Ronnie, she said to herself, but she was certain the other dragons heard.

The third dragon arrived and joined the melee against Ronnie.

Today, we shall kill a king," Rembert said.

The two dragons used their weight to pull Ronnie to the canyon floor as his wings struggled to keep him aloft.

She said the magick words aloud, and the power rushed from her, leaving her feeling deflated.

Ronnie flew back into view, separated from the other dragons.

They darted at him, and each time they neared his body, they slowed and dropped away. They kept attacking, but less frequently as Ronnie circled high in the sky.

The two older dragons looked at her. Missy braced for whatever they had in mind. While they were distracted, Ronnie dove and wrapped his jaws around Rembert's neck. They wrestled, their two necks entwined like snakes.

And then Rembert went limp. He and Ronnie fell from the sky.

While the other dragon flew straight at the van.

Missy had no choice but to take her concentration away from Ronnie's protection spell. She frantically attempted to build one around the van. With the spell for Ronnie already built, she tried to alter it for its new purpose rather than rebuild it from scratch.

The dragon zoomed toward her. Dragon eyes, she mused as she prepared to die, had vertical pupils like cat eyes.

The dragon slammed into the van.

And the protection spell saved it from being crushed and sliced open. But it didn't stop the van from being knocked off the top of the plateau.

It fell toward the canyon floor upside down, with Missy pressed against the floor.

THE PROTECTION SPELL should protect the van when it hit the rocky ground, but Missy would be tossed about like a rag doll inside it.

She wouldn't survive.

She struggled to think amid her panic. It came to her quickly: she could weave a spirit web.

She flung every bit of energy she had from her solar plexus, tiny tendrils of power entwined like a spider web, meant to catch souls, ghosts, and dreams. She fortified it with ectoplasm so it could hold her body mass, as well.

There was no time to test it.

The van hit the rocks, the protection bubble flexing but holding firm. With a spine-snapping jolt, the van, ensconced in its bubble, bounced like a tennis ball. The gravity, that tried to smash Missy against the roof of the van, suddenly yanked her in the opposite direction as the van shot upwards after it bounced.

Missy, jerked back and forth, hung safely suspended, for now, in her spirit net.

The van dropped again, a shorter distance this time, and bounced once more.

Missy had a brief glimpse of the body of Rembert lying atop a boulder before the van in its bubble careened away, hitting the wall of the plateau.

After a series of smaller bounces, the van settled upon the canyon floor. The interior was bathed in light from a fireball above. Ronnie was battling the other dragon lord.

She broke the spirit web and crawled from the van to establish a visual connection with Ronnie.

Two dragons came into view, wrestling, tails whipping, they crashed into the side of the canyon sending rubble falling that just missed her.

She fixed her eyes upon Ronnie and carefully transferred the protection spell to him. Strand by strand, layer by layer, pulse by pulse, she rebuilt it around him.

The two dragons sprung apart as the bubble formed around Ronnie. The lord flung himself at Ronnie but couldn't get close enough to make contact.

An eruption of flame danced across the bubble's surface, leaving Ronnie unharmed.

He went in for the kill. The talons on his four limbs sank into the dragon lord's abdomen as he was pushed against the canyon wall. He was held there as Ronnie finished the evisceration.

The lifeless body of the dragon lord dropped to the rubble only thirty feet from where the van lay, causing a cloud of dust and pebbles.

Missy, are you all right? Ronnie's voice asked in her head.

He landed on a nearby boulder and looked her over. He was covered with blood, his own and the other dragons'. Several scales were missing, and a gash ran along the length of his neck.

Could be better, she said. *What about you? You must be in great pain.*

Your magick. You protected me while somehow saving yourself. I didn't think earth magick could be so strong in the In Between.

I'm surprised myself. I had more reserves of energy in my core than I thought possible. Maybe it was because I'm inspired by you.

I could have beaten Rembert and Foss one to one, but not together, he said in an effort to repair his male pride. *They're bigger than me, but I'm younger. I didn't want it to come to this, but it's just as well. Some dragons are only impressed by brute force. I had been trying to accommodate the opinions of the elders, but many saw it as a sign of weakness.*

What are you going to do now?

Each of the lords I just killed led a clan that must be convinced to give me their loyalty. First, I need to meet with the other lords of the council and make them reaffirm their fealty to me. I might have to kill one or two more.

Do you need my magick?

I need to do this on my own. You won't always be here to bail me out.

Missy was relieved. Her inner reserves of energy were nearly tapped out. She doubted she had enough to create another effective protection spell.

As I reassert my authority over the council, I will declare a unilateral truce between reptiles and humanoids. The Bill-devil is dead, but you need to make sure other humans and vampires don't attack us.

The dragons must stop showing up where they can be seen.

We will try. And humanoids need to stop making up crazy conspiracy theories.

We will try, Missy said, though she knew her species was doomed to continue dabbling in self-destructive fantasies.

I will send a gateway to you very soon. I'm sorry you and I found each other on opposite sides of this conflict.

We'll stay friends, she said. *Be sure to see a healer right away about those wounds.*

He smiled a toothy dragon smile.

I will. And we will. Remain friends, that is. Until we meet again, Missy.

He flapped his massive wings and ascended from the canyon. Only a few minutes later, a circular area of shimmering air moved across the canyon floor toward her. As it neared, she felt the usual nausea and anxiety. But she gladly stepped through the gateway. She was eager to return home.

A CASUAL OFFER

The moment Missy stepped out of the gateway and into her living room, she was greeted by her two gray tabbies, Brenda and Bubba. They were showing genuine affection, not just demanding to be fed.

She looked in the kitchen. The cat dishes contained half-eaten, but fresh, food.

"Someone's been feeding you," she said. "Did Matt come by?"

They answered by rubbing themselves against her legs, their tails sticking upward in happiness. Matt had a spare key and was often her cat sitter.

The toilet flushed in the guest bathroom to confirm her assumption.

Matt walked out into the living room. His face lit up with joy when he saw her.

"Thank God you're all right and back," he said, giving her a big hug that picked her off the floor. "Why couldn't you return with me?"

"The dragon lords used me as a hostage to exchange for Bill. Long story. The good news is that Ronnie is consolidating power and calling off the war with humans and vampires."

"What a relief," Matt said.

His arms were still around her. She realized she didn't mind it so much. But she backed away before things got out of hand.

He frowned. "I wasn't making moves on you. It just felt comfortable being close to you."

"Yeah. It did."

"Maybe we should do it more often," he said with a wiggle of his eyebrows.

"I wouldn't want you to get the wrong idea."

"What kind of idea is wrong?"

"We've been friends for a long time," she said. "I care about you a lot."

He frowned again. "I don't need to hear the 'you're like a brother to me' speech."

"No, not like a brother. That would be illegal in most states."

"What are you talking about?"

"Matt, I find you sexy, as well as fun to be with. I wouldn't mind taking the fun to another level. But I'm not ready for a relationship right now. I feel that I'm in a transitional stage of my life. It's not the right time for me to fall in love."

"There's never a right or wrong time. It just happens," he said.

"I guess I don't want it to happen right now."

"So, what exactly are you suggesting? A friends-with-benefits arrangement?"

"Possibly. We're far from being innocent kids anymore."

He folded his arms and took a step backwards. "I don't know."

She was confused. "I've felt the electricity between us."

"Yes. But I also have, well, feelings for you. More than just fondness. Do you understand?"

"Yes. I'm sorry, but my feelings haven't quite gotten that far yet. But they could. Just not right now."

"That's the problem," he said.

"It doesn't have to be a problem."

"It is for me. Because of my feelings, I'm more vulnerable than you. I can't just hang out, have a little hanky-panky, and go about my business like it's no big deal. I want to dive headfirst into a relationship. A love affair."

Missy was quiet. She'd known he had feelings for her, which was why she'd never thought intimacy was possible. She didn't want to hurt him if she couldn't reciprocate the feelings. But she believed it would be possible to add the physical aspect without too much attachment.

"It's not too much to ask for love," Matt said. "I've never been married before, like you. I still have idealistic notions of how it could be. I believe I'm not too old to be a dad. You're not too old to have a child."

"I'm not at the stage of life yet when I'm ready to make marriage work again. The first one didn't go so well."

Her husband left her for a vampire and was staked not long after he was turned. Her idealistic views of marriage had been left far behind. And as far as children, she still had the occasional pang of missing being a mother. But face it, her life was so weird now—so deep into magick and monsters that being a soccer mom seemed impossible. And how could she raise a child when her life was in danger as often as the electric bill was due?

"You just want to use me for my body," Matt said.

"I sure do!" She was happy to return to talk of shallow pleasure.

She smiled.

He struggled not to, but broke into a grin.

"It's impossible to pout around you," he said.

"Good. I hate pouters."

"Well, your proposition is certainly worth considering. I need to decide if I want to risk getting hurt."

"It doesn't hurt if you do it right."

"You know what I mean!"

"It is rather awkward talking about these things in the abstract," she said.

"Yes. It's a little easier if you get me drunk and 'these things' happen naturally."

"Remind me to keep my fridge stocked with your favorite beer."

"And I'll be sure to limit my consumption, so I don't get taken advantage of. Anyway, I need to run," he said. "I've been assigned a follow-up story about Bill's murder. The authorities are still puzzled why his dead body turned into dust."

He gave her a quick kiss on the cheek and left.

Speaking of vampires, Missy had several voicemails and texts from Agnes on her phone, now that it was working again. And as she scrolled down, she was horrified to find messages from the van-rental agency.

She was overdue for returning the van. The van that lay upside down at the bottom of a canyon in another plane of existence.

Oh, my.

Missy's absences to San Marcos and the In Between had created a backlog of patient visits. A sweet, elderly male troll, who lived in a small apartment building at the foot of the Intracoastal Waterway bridge, needed his annual physical. She told him he should watch his weight and exercise more. After becoming too old to snatch and eat people crossing the bridge, he had switched to a typical high-calorie, high-fat American diet. She hated to be a scold, but overweight trolls had a high incidence of heart disease.

Next, she visited two different werewolf patients at Seaweed Manor on the beach. They also needed to lose weight. She recommended they go on longer runs as a pack every night they shifted to wolves. The werewolves in this community were also notorious for partying. There was always the smell of weed drifting through the hallways. She reminded her patients to moderate their drinking. Werewolves didn't make suitable candidates for liver transplants.

Finally, once nightfall had set in, she went next door to Squid Tower. She had three vampire patients who needed routine screenings. Blood draws were always a dangerous procedure with vampires, but she gritted her teeth, put on her warding amulet, and did her job.

She stopped by Agnes' condo before going home.

"I'm relieved you're okay," Agnes said, hugging her. The old vampire was so petite her head only came up to Missy's belly.

"Is the community in shock over Bill's death?" Missy asked.

"I hate to say it, but there's a sense of relief. He used to make everyone nervous with all his guns. And once he got into conspiracy theories, he was like a bomb about to go off. Oops, poor choice of words."

"The creative writing class I teach is next week. It will be strange without him and his war fiction."

"Speaking of war, if Ronnie honors what he promised you, our conflict with the dragons is, thankfully, over. But another one is building with the police."

"Detective Affird?"

"Yes. He made it clear to me he knows we're vampires," Agnes said. "He's gone from suspicion to certainty. And he's coping with having seen the dragons that night you were kidnapped."

"With luck, he'll never see another dragon again, and there won't be anything he can do about them."

"Yes. But we need to deal with him. I've sent a notice to all residents to avoid feeding on humans, at least for several weeks. We need to lie low and not give him any provocation. I don't believe he would simply attack our community and stake everyone. But if he had to come here on police business, he very well could leave some staked vampires behind."

"Oh, my."

"That is, unless we take a more proactive approach."

"Like what? Wait, don't tell me. I don't want to know."

ON MISSY'S WAY HOME, she stopped at MegaMart, since it was open until midnight. She picked up cat food and human food, in that order of importance. As she passed through the home goods section, she spotted a man who looked familiar. He was examining a pair of dusting slippers. Until now, Missy hadn't known she could dust her floors while shuffling around in her slippers.

The man looked exactly like Marvin.

But, of course, it couldn't be him. Overweight, older men tend to look the same, even if they're vampires. She turned around and passed the aisle again to get a better look.

The man turned his back and was studying a shelf of garden gnomes.

She circled around the rows of shelves to pass the other end of the aisle. But then an employee rolled a cart of boxes, blocking her and her view. By the time she navigated to a better position, the man had disappeared.

He had really looked like Marvin, although she hadn't seen his face straight on. She obviously was mistaken. Marvin was dead. She'd seen the pile of ashes he'd become.

Besides, Marvin lived at Squid Tower. The HOA bylaws would never allow a garden gnome to be displayed outdoors. The man had to be a human, not Marvin.

But why did he look so much like Marvin?

She was beginning to think like one of the crazy conspiracy theorists. This had to stop.

Still, she wandered through the entire MegaMart, from auto parts to underwear, looking for the man. He was nowhere to be found.

Could that have been Marvin's ghost she saw? She had to think about that for a few minutes. Did vampires even become ghosts? Weren't they already undead? And if it was his ghost, why would he be haunting the home goods section of MegaMart?

Her brain hurt, so she tried to think about trivial things as she finished her shopping. But ghost or not, the sighting continued to haunt her.

Finally, she broke down and called Agnes.

"Does Marvin's neighbor, Mrs. Kinkuddy, still have that bag of ashes she said she collected from Marvin's lounge chair?"

"I believe so," Agnes said. "Detective Affird never came by to collect them. I believe he's certain it was a case of a vampire being sun-torched. He was only pretending to believe otherwise."

"I need to get those ashes."

"Why would you want to do that?"

"I'll explain later."

AGNES USED a spare set of keys to let Missy into Marvin's condo. With no living heirs to leave it to, he apparently willed it to the Flat Earth Society. It hadn't passed through probate yet.

Missy needed a favorite possession of Marvin's to make the spell work. On his desk, next to the oversized monitor and pile of conspiracy-theory books, was a framed selfie of Marvin posing with his face near a footprint in the mud. Presumably, it was a Reptilian footprint, but it looked more like it was left by a tipsy bear. She grabbed the photo and began drawing a magic circle on the kitchen tile with a dry-erase marker.

"I'll leave you alone so you can concentrate," Agnes said with a dubious expression.

Modern science had difficulty identifying a person through their ashes in the absence of bone fragments. The incineration process destroys all traces of DNA. The only other method is reading X-ray emissions by using a particle accelerator.

Magick had better means. Missy considered magick a form of science that scientists refused, or were unable, to understand.

To explain her spell in simple terms, she harvested Marvin's psychic energy, traces of which were left as a residue on things he touched, particularly a beloved object.

Her spell would "analyze"—to use a scientific word—his ashes to look for matching psychic energy. The heat of incineration can't destroy this energy, unlike DNA.

She completed her circle, placed five tea candles in the points of a pentagram. A grill lighter lit the candles. Then, she began gathering her energies and those from the five elements, particularly water, since the ocean was just outside. Her own energies were still weak from overusing them in the In Between.

The spell was one that Don Mateo had devised, combining principles of alchemy, earth magick, and the magic of the original inhabitants of Florida. She read the incantation from a notecard, a curious jumble of Latin, Old English, and Timucuan.

The picture frame glowed along its edges as she activated and extracted Marvin's psychic energy.

Next, she transferred that energy to the searching part of the spell. The plastic baggy of ashes grew warm in her hands. She expected it to become uncomfortably hot, with a spiritual heat, not the kind that would melt the plastic bag. But the bag remained simply warm.

The image of Marvin's face she expected to see did not enter her mind. Instead, she saw only a black silhouette of a man.

The ashes must not belong to Marvin. Another man had been torched on Marvin's balcony, not him. Who the man was, Missy couldn't tell. Though the psychic energy was similar to Marvin's.

He had been a very close friend. Or, more likely, he had been a family member. But as far as Missy knew, Marvin lived alone and didn't have living relatives.

While the spell was still active, Missy lifted the baggy of ashes, rotating her arm around the room. She hoped to use the process in reverse, trying to match the unidentified psychic energy in the ashes with an object in the condo.

Not until the bag was closest to the second bedroom did something happen, a slight electric jolt to her fingers.

The ashes belonged to someone with a recent connection to that bedroom.

Leaving the magick circle broke the spell. But she carried the baggy into the bedroom. A vampire slept in here. The room, the bed in particular, gave her the creepy tingly feeling she had whenever she was in a vampire patient's bedroom. Which she tried to do as little as possible.

She smelled a man's old-fashioned hair tonic. The closet and dresser held men's out-of-fashion clothing. No personal items were visible. It truly felt as if whoever slept in here had been a guest.

Then, she noticed the oddest thing. A deadbolt had been installed. On the outside of the door.

Was the occupant of this room Marvin's prisoner?

Marvin had become even creepier in her eyes. And he apparently wasn't dead. This vampire prisoner was most likely the one who had been sun-torched on the balcony.

But why? To allow Marvin to live a secret life of garden-gnome shopping at MegaMart?

She called Agnes.

"Did Marvin have anyone staying with him in his condo?"

"Not that I know of," Agnes said. "Marvin was a very solitary fellow. No living human relatives. I don't believe he kept in touch with his maker. Why do you ask?"

Missy explained her findings.

"Perhaps, he took in another conspiracy buff who needed a place to stay."

It didn't ring right to Missy.

"Thank you. I'll be here a while longer, seeing if I can find out more."

"Lock the door on your way out."

Missy decided to try her spell again. She used the tube of hair tonic on the guest bedroom dresser to provide the psychic energy.

Repeating the spell, she held the baggy of ashes as it grew warmer, then hotter, like it was supposed to. This time, an image of a face appeared in her mind.

Marvin's face.

What the heck?

So, these were, in fact, Marvin's ashes? It had been Marvin who was sun-torched on his balcony, after all?

Okay.

But why was he imprisoned in his own guest bedroom?

She searched the master bedroom. She found an old address book that was surely Marvin's, with yellowed pages and many addresses in a pre-modern format, such as only a name, street number, and no zip code or telephone number. Other listings had four-digit phone numbers. Marvin's name was written on the inside front cover.

She repeated the spell. The book was rich with psychic energy. And it matched again with the ashes. It was more confirmation that Marvin had been the victim, as everyone assumed.

So why was he sleeping in his guest bedroom? Was he really locked in here? Probably, whoever locked him in this room was the one who locked him on his balcony to be sun-torched.

More and more vampires suspected Bill was Marvin's murderer. Missy was inclined to agree.

And she realized she had been mistaken when she thought she saw Marvin in the MegaMart.

STAKING TIME

Detective Fred Affird had unfinished business.

The lunatic militia that called itself ERR was imploding. Their leader, the vampire Bill Meany, was dead. His murderer, Abe Washington, was under arrest. The rest of them had gone underground, which was just fine with Affird. The organization had been decapitated, the actual gunmen who had fired upon the police were dead, and the rest of the militia was not his problem. Let the FBI or ATF worry about them. Affird had bigger fish to fry.

For instance, what was he going to do about the dragons?

He had fabricated a story for the incident report stating the militants had accidentally torched themselves with gasoline bombs. The other officers at the scene, who saw the dragons, were keeping it to themselves for the time being, not wanting to be thought crazy. Affird, and all the superior officers, denied that dragons exist and asserted, therefore, that no one could have seen them.

There had been no reported sighting of dragons since then. Hopefully, there wouldn't be, and Affird could make himself forget they existed.

What remained unsettled was the vampire question. Affird was ready to wipe them out, once and for all.

No, not all of them. He'd promised his informant, Mrs. Kinkuddy, that he would keep her from being staked if she continued to give him information about Squid Tower.

He had suspected the community was filled with vampires for the longest time but couldn't do anything about it. Not even with the information his informant had given him. Now, however, he was ready to act.

It was time to send the message they were not welcome in Jellyfish Beach. If they didn't move away, they would be staked. He would set an example by staking their leaders.

There was also the problem with the werewolves living next door in Seaweed Manor. Most of the time, those residents were in human form, so they were less of an open sore for Affird than the vampires were. He had killed one of them before, but almost lost his badge for trying to kill an old lady werewolf who raised a stink with the department.

He wouldn't mind ignoring that problem like the dragons.

The vampires were his focus. It's why he made a late-night visit to Squid Tower to help him plan his attack.

As usual, the community was buzzing with activity at 10:30 p.m., which was not the case with any human retirement village, that's for sure. The pickleball courts were busy with doubles matches. The shuffleboard courts were occupied. Pale vampires in bathing suits crowded the pool.

They didn't make the slightest effort to hide their nocturnal lives. They had grown too confident they wouldn't be discovered.

First, Affird rang the bell at the condo of Oleg Kazmirov.

"Good evening, Detective," Oleg said at the door. "How can I help you?"

"Do you have a few minutes? I have some follow-up questions about the militia."

The Russian vampire nodded grimly. It looked like he had wrongly believed his militia problems were behind him.

Affird walked in and looked around. The front door had a normal locking doorknob and a simple deadbolt. A battering ram should make quick work of it.

"Have a seat, Detective," Oleg said as he sat in a wingback chair.

"Thanks, but I won't be long. Have you had any further contact with the militia?"

"No, sir."

Affird made note of the master bedroom's location. He glanced inside it to see the layout. No coffin in here, just a bed. He memorized where it was.

The key to staking vampires was to catch them unaware. Affird and his tactical team would have to bust into the condo, without knocking, during daylight hours, race to the bedroom, and drive a stake into the creature's heart before he had awakened enough to fight back.

Affird had two men whom he trusted to share his secret about vampires and keep the raid secret. He seriously doubted the vampires would report it. But if they did, he would concoct a plausible cover story.

"Did you speak to Bill Meany after the attack in Alligator Hammock?"

"No. I was disillusioned by him. Disgusted, actually," the vampire said in a thick Russian accent. "I only joined the militia because I shared Bill's love of shooting, and he really wanted me to join. I didn't want any violence. And Bill, he really lost his mind. He wouldn't have spoken to me, anyway. He believed I betrayed him."

Affird didn't ask why Oleg had gone to Alligator Hammock in the first place. When Affird questioned him that night, there had been a mention of a baby dragon. Affird didn't want to talk about dragons anymore.

Affird made note of where the vampire's gun cabinet was in the living room. An antique cavalry sword was displayed on the wall. The vampire might have a handgun in his bedside table. Body armor would be required for this raid.

"Do you know of any future operations the militia has planned?"

"I'm not aware of any plans," the vampire said.

Affird was done here. No more meaningless questions. The vampire didn't know this yet, but the D.A. was not bringing any charges against him.

"Thank you for your time, Mr. Kazmirov. Have a good evening."

Next, he visited Sol Felderberg. This vampire was late in answering the door. The television was turned up so loudly, it probably took a while before he heard the bell and the knocking.

Affird had believed all vampires had superhuman hearing. Not this old geezer.

"Come in, come in," Sol said after he finally opened the door. "I'm binge-watching *Desperate Housewives of Albuquerque*. You ever watch this?"

"No,"

Sol plopped down on his couch. Unlike the Russian, this guy really looked like a vampire, with his deathly white bald head and pointy ears. Kind of like the one in that old movie, *Nosferatu*.

Affird asked the vampire the same questions he had asked the Russian while he surveyed the condo. Same locks on the front door. The bedroom was pretty weird, though. There was no bed, no furniture at all. Just a stone crypt in the middle of the floor with its lid open.

A paperback book and reading glasses lay on the floor next to the crypt. It was a vampire romance novel.

Affird worried the vampire closed the stone lid of the crypt when he slept. He made a note to bring crowbars, just in case, to pop the lid open before staking the monster.

The vampire was laughing in the living room at the television.

"That manipulative little brat!" Mr. Felderberg said.

While he asked more rote questions about the militia, Affird scoped out any possible weapons in the condo. He saw none, but assumed they existed. The only decoration in the place was Boston Red Sox memorabilia. A photo of Felderberg posing in historical clothing next to a horse and buggy was the only exception to the baseball theme. Pretty cocky to hang such an old picture of himself, showing guests how old he really was.

But Sol wasn't self-conscious about it. He continued to concentrate on the television program.

"Thank you for your time, Mr. Felderberg," Affird said as he left.

It was time to visit the supreme leader of the vampires, the president of the HOA.

He'd been in Agnes' condo before. It was large and tastefully decorated. There were signs someone else lived here, as well. He asked about that.

"Maria."

"Maria Cavallos? The one who was at the gun battle in Alligator Hammock?"

Agnes nodded.

"Is she here right now?"

"No. She's out doing whatever young women do these days."

"I see."

Affird figured she was out hunting. Assaulting innocent humans. She would have to be staked, as well. Two vampires in one condo presented a problem, though. They would have to be staked simultaneously, or the one not yet staked would wake up and attack Affird and his men. He would have to increase his team by at least one more member, so there would be two of them for each vampire in this residence.

Affird asked his stock questions while he paced around the condo, trying to look like he was wandering aimlessly. Agnes wasn't buying it. She followed him around, using her quad cane.

"Are you looking for anything?" she asked.

"Walking helps me think."

"That's what some people say. At my age, walking only makes me hurt."

Affird smiled. She was a charming little lady, but a monster, nonetheless. He looked forward to staking her.

"Detective, I've told you everything about the militia. I hope they disband. Oleg and Sol want nothing to do with them."

"That's good to hear. But I have additional open business here at Squid Tower. Has anyone heard from the nurse, Missy Mindle?"

"I just saw her last night. She's doing well."

"Did she return the rental van that's missing?"

"I wouldn't know."

"Was she at Alligator Hammock on the night in question?"

"I don't believe she was. You must have seen a different rental van."

"And there's the man who was burned to death upstairs," Affird said. "That case needs to be closed."

"You never picked up the ashes that his neighbor collected."

"I didn't? I must have been too busy."

Affird believed from the start that the incinerated man had been a vampire destroyed by the sun. He hadn't planned to waste time investigating it. The death was merely an excuse to spend more time unmasking the vampires here.

"Are you working the overnight shift, Detective? It seems awfully late for you to come here with routine questions. I believe you'll find the overnight shift will suit you well in the future."

Affird was noting the bedrooms. The master was normal-looking, though the bed was small and old-fashioned. Two guest rooms were on the opposite side of the floor plan. The one on the right was clearly being used, though the young vampire had almost no possessions.

The condo had a security system, however. He had noticed a doorbell camera, and an alarm keypad was on the kitchen wall. They would need to raid this unit after the vampire men were staked to lessen the amount of time the alarm was sounding.

The little old vampire kept following him around. She was suspicious. You don't survive as a vampire for as long as she has without being canny.

"Detective, is there something else you need from me?"

"Not at the moment, Mrs. Geberich. Thank you for your . . ."

He was drawn to her eyes. They were fascinating. She had an odd expression on her face, but he couldn't tear his eyes away from hers. They were gray and beautiful, somewhat bloodshot, but still powerful. Intense. And wise, so wise.

"Detective, you look tired," she said. "Please sit down."

He sat down at the kitchen table without thinking. Sitting down was something he truly needed, wanted, to do. But why?

The old-lady vampire spoke to him continually in a smooth, mellifluous voice, while her eyes remained locked to his. He listened carefully because what she said was so important. It was life-changing.

She pulled a chair next to his and sat very close while her wise words rolled over him like water. No, like blood. Like a babbling brook of pure, innocent blood.

"You're such a large man, and I am so small," she said, her face close to his. He never let go of her eyes. "How will I ever drink so much blood?"

Of course, he thought, she was a vampire. What else would she do but drink my blood? He wasn't the least bit frightened, just eager to please. He surprised himself by leaning toward her, cocking his head, and offering her the side of his neck.

He closed his eyes.

The fangs didn't hurt that much. In fact, the wounds itched a bit. His heart slowed down and matched the rhythm of her steady gulps. She continued drinking without a pause, while something inside his head buzzed like a cicada, and his breaths grew shallow.

"Are you going to kill me?" he asked.

She paused her drinking. "You must die to be reborn to eternal life."

He realized this was how new vampires were made.

"If I die, will I lose my pension?"

"You won't be dead. You'll be undead."

The undead detective. It had a nice ring to it.

That was his last thought before he lost consciousness.

When he awoke, he lay on his back on the kitchen floor. Something was in his mouth. It was the skinny arm of Agnes, and he was drinking blood from it. He felt very strange. Something irrevocable had changed in him and in his life.

He pushed the arm from his mouth.

"What happened to me?"

"Before I tell you, what is your age?"

"Fifty-six."

"Congratulations, Detective Affird. You meet both criteria to become a resident of Squid Tower."

Missy stopped by Agnes' place to say goodbye before she headed up to San Marcos to continue her investigation. That's when she learned Agnes had turned Affird.

It was a huge relief to know he wouldn't be a threat anymore. But Missy found the living arrangements odd at Agnes' condo. A ninety-something woman in body years (1,500 in actual years), lived with a twenty-six-year-old newly made vampire woman, and a newly made vampire cop who was fifty-six.

It was like the concept for a bad television sitcom.

"Fred will move back to his house," Agnes said, "once he's finished his transition. He needs a lot of supervision until then."

"Which I never had when I was turned," Maria said, brooding.

"Neither did I, dear," Agnes said. "No one said becoming a vampire was easy."

Affird sat on the couch, staring at Missy with zombie eyes. He clearly had much more transitioning to do.

"It will be so nice having a police officer who understands us and protects our interests," Agnes said. "Right, Freddie?"

Affird grunted

"Maybe he'll even sell his house and buy a place at Squid Tower. It's a great place to spend eternity."

Affird grunted. Missy was sure she saw a smile crease his fang-creased lips.

"Ocean view," he said in a dead voice.

18

I'LL HAVE MY DEMON CALL YOURS

The archives of the Magic Guild of San Marcos were not kept in a Gothic-inspired library of dark, polished wood. Nor were they in a dungeon keep. They were in an air-conditioned self-storage facility next to an industrial park. She followed Wendall's car there.

The records Missy sought were in a giant, leather-bound book. Several volumes dating back to the late fifteen hundreds chronicled important rules or decisions handed down by the Guild. They filled several metal shelves that packed the room.

When Missy reached the section that covered the year of her birth, she scanned the entries, hand-written in elegant cursive with a fine-point fountain pen.

The name leaped out. "Ophelia Lawthorne. Excommunicated from the Guild on the Ninth of July for activities involving black magic. Banished from the city and county on the Thirtieth of November, never to return under threat of death by stoning."

Oh, my. This was hardcore stuff. She flipped randomly through subsequent pages. The entries varied from the seriousness of her mother's sentence to rules outlawing certain spells or requiring the purity of ingredients in others. Notices of members with unpaid dues. An announcement of an upcoming picnic and raffle.

Then: "Special meeting called to discuss resurgence of black magic." Later, a mention outlawing the organization of any subgroups studying black magic.

The announcement of her father's death stood out like a bloodstain: "Theodore Lawthorne, murdered by a demon. His infant daughter shall be given by adoption to the nearest kin. The infant's mother, Ophelia Lawthorne, is forbidden to have custody of the child pursuant to the Guild's ruling that she is unfit for motherhood."

It was like a smack in the face to see the unhappy tidings of her family written in black ink in such stark terms.

The next entry stated that a demonologist commissioned by the Guild determined the demon who killed her father was Asmodeus.

On the next pages, mixed in with the mundane listings, were mentions of other demonic activity and additional members of the Guild banished for practicing black magic.

There was quite a wave of black magic at the time. She wondered why.

Soon, she came upon a statement that Tommy Albinoni, working as a special investigator, cleared Ophelia Lawthorne of the accusations she was behind her husband's murder. Who the actual culprit was remained undetermined. It referenced the full report published elsewhere.

A few pages later, other entries grabbed her attention. Both

Tommy Albinoni and Eliza-May Jenkins were excommunicated for experimenting with black magic together.

Missy thought it odd that the two were mentioned as working together, as if they were a couple. Eliza-May had mentioned her boyfriend had been a rival to Ted. She claimed her boyfriend was dead. What if she was lying and her boyfriend was Albinoni?

It didn't say they were banished, however. Further down the page, it said they were taking remedial instruction to cleanse themselves of evil remnants.

This was after Albinoni investigated Missy's father's death. But not long after.

She looked up to catch Wendall staring at her, leaning against the doorway to the storage unit.

"How do we know Tommy Albinoni wasn't involved with black magic when he investigated my mother?" she asked.

"We don't know. When he investigated her, his integrity was beyond question. But when we later found out about his secret violation of the magic code, no one went back to double-check his findings."

"He could have been in league with my mother, or sympathetic to her, at the very least."

"Perhaps."

"So, let's say his report was fabricated or just wrong. It still leaves me where I started: suspecting Ophelia summoned the demon but having no proof of it. Albinoni won't tell me the truth. I don't think my truth-telling spell would work on him."

"It wouldn't," Wendall said with a wry smile. "Not on a wizard of his level."

"Who else can I talk to?"

"The demon."

"What did you just say?"

"Talk to the demon himself. Who would know better than he? How you're going to summon Asmodeus is an open question. I can't help you do that. No one in the Guild could. You'd probably die trying to do it."

Missy knew the perfect person to do it.

Ex-Father Marco Rivera Hernandez had been known as an expert demonologist and exorcist. Unfortunately, he met his match with one demon he tried to expel from an adolescent girl. The demon left the girl but possessed the priest instead. With the demon inside him, Father Marco committed several serious gaffes, including interrupting Mass and desecrating the altar. He once rained poop on a charity golf tournament. Most of the time, the demon did relatively harmless pranks, like taking over the priest long enough for him to say offensive things, before quickly disappearing and leaving the priest to endure the humiliation.

Ex-Father Marco's most serious offense while under the demon's influence was revealing evidence the bishop was embezzling funds from his diocese. For this, more so than the demon itself, Marco was defrocked and excommunicated.

These days, he worked as a blackjack dealer at a Native American casino.

Missy once battled a demon who had possessed the garden gnomes of Jellyfish Beach. Ex-Father Marco's demon identified this other demon for Missy.

It turned out, of course, that the gnome-possessing demon had been summoned by her mother for a paying client.

"So, you want my demon to talk to Asmodeus and find out who summoned him to kill your father?" Marco asked.

"Exactly."

"You do know that demons are notorious for lying, right?"

"Lying to humans. Maybe Asmodeus would tell the truth to your demon. You know, if they hit it off."

"He would know the information was requested by a human."

"Well, it's not a perfect plan, but it's the only one I've got."

"I'll see what I can do."

It didn't hurt that the former priest had the hots for her. Missy was guilty of taking advantage of that, but she never manipulated the man. She simply allowed his sinfulness to do its thing.

Missy drove back to Jellyfish Beach, putting yet more miles on her much-abused car. She couldn't demand the former priest drive all the way to San Marcos.

She also needed to use her home to host the demon encounter. She didn't know what else to call it. It wasn't exactly a seance. Nor was it a summoning using magic. It was more of a demonic meet-and-greet.

Did she need to serve hors d'oeuvres for this?

When Matt found out about it, he insisted on being invited. He offered to bring craft beer and pretzels. It truly was turning into a demon party.

Ex-Father Marco showed up at 8:30 p.m. on a night Missy didn't have any patient home visits. The former priest, who had a trimmed beard and looked like a Spanish nobleman from a Renaissance painting, had a troubled look on his face.

"I can't guarantee my demon will cooperate. Or even show

up at all. His primary purpose seems to be to embarrass me and ruin my life."

Marco's face went blank.

"You really think my purpose has anything to do with you?" he spoke in a nasal, high-pitched voice as if he'd just inhaled helium. It was his demon speaking. "A ruined priest with no career is my main focus? Get out of here. I've got my fingers in a lot of pies bigger than you."

"What is your name?" Matt asked.

"Clarence."

"That's not a typical demon name."

"Exactly. It's not a typical, overused, boring name like Matt."

"Clarence, can you help us by speaking to another demon?" Missy asked. "A specific one?"

"It's not like I have every demon in my contacts list." Now he had a deep voice like a 1950s TV announcer. "There are a whole lot of demons in Hell and on earth. Way more than Lucifer's army. There are new ones created every day. Some people going to Hell lately are so evil they get promoted almost immediately to demons."

"The demon we wish to contact is one of the old-school ones. Asmodeus is his name."

"You're right. He's way old school. And even if I found him, I don't know if I'd be allowed to speak with him. Exactly why should I even entertain the idea of helping you?"

"To impress us with how powerful you are," Matt said.

Good one, Missy thought.

"Very true," the demon said.

Life returned to Marco's face.

"Did the demon take me over?" he asked.

Missy and Matt nodded.

"It sounds like he's going to look for Asmodeus," Missy said.

"We'll see about that. Never trust him. I would—"

Marco's face went blank again.

"I'm back!" Clarence announced flamboyantly. "I spoke to Asmodeus' assistant. I need to tell him what this is in reference to. He won't answer any questions about tax fraud."

"We want to know who summoned him forty-three years ago when he killed a powerful witch named Ted Lawthorne."

"Okey-dokey."

The ex-priest's cognitive abilities returned. "Anything?"

"No," Missy said. "Not yet. Clarence is trying to get through Hell's bureaucracy."

"Good luck with that. This is making me very uncomfortable, by the way, with the demon repeatedly entering me and then leaving."

"I'm sorry," Missy said.

"Want a beer?" Matt asked.

Marco nodded. After Matt handed him an uncapped bottle, he took a long drink.

And spit the beer on Matt.

A fiendish giggling came from the now slack-faced Marco.

"I thought demons were evil," Matt said. "This one's just childish."

"Depends on your definition of evil," the demon said in his helium voice. "Good news: Asmodeus has agreed to speak with me. Looks like I still got some juice in Hell, baby."

"Please ask who summoned him to kill Ted Lawthorne," Missy said.

All the lights in the house went out. The walls rumbled like a freight train was passing through. Lightning flashes appeared in the windows.

"I was summoned," said a voice in a hoarse whisper that was deafeningly loud for a whisper, "by the black-magic sorceress Ophelia."

"My mother," Missy said. "I was actually hoping it hadn't been her."

"But I was not summoned to kill her husband," Asmodeus' voice said. "Ophelia commanded me to steal something from the house and return it to her."

"Ask him what it was," Missy said.

More rumbling in the walls.

"I was commanded to steal an infant girl from her crib and deliver her to Ophelia. But the male witch tried to intervene. He tried to stop me with magic. I am too powerful to be stopped by a mere mortal who plays at magic. And once I am summoned, I obey only my summoner."

"What happened to my father?"

"I killed him because he annoyed me. I used a dishwasher so it would look like an accident."

"No one gets killed in household dishwasher accidents," Matt said.

He screamed when a bolt of electricity hit him, leaving his hair standing on end.

"When I killed the witch, I lost my focus," Asmodeus said. "I'm easily distracted. The summoning was broken, and I returned to Hell. I did not complete the task I had been assigned. But I did kill someone, so all in all, it was a good night."

"Thanks, for the info," Missy said in a soft voice.

She was stunned. It was as if her world had been turned upside down again, after it had been upended when she first learned about her adoption and losing her birth parents.

Now her mother didn't seem quite as evil as before. Still evil, but not as bad.

She wanted me with her, Missy thought. She had the tiniest trace of a motherly instinct after all.

She reminded herself that her mother had been willing to kill her since then. But adult children aren't as adorable as when they were babies, so maybe it was understandable.

"Did you get an answer?" Marco asked, back in control of his body and mind.

"Yes. Not the one I was expecting, though."

"Maybe you should get your mom something for Mother's Day this year," Matt said.

"Do we know if Asmodeus was telling the truth?" she asked the ex-priest after she explained what she had learned.

"You never know for sure with a demon," Marco said. "In my experience as an exorcist, I found the older demons didn't lie as much as the younger ones. When they lied, it was for a purpose, like getting me to stop the exorcism. Not misleading to no end."

"Why hasn't she told me the truth about this?" Missy asked. "She wanted me to donate a kidney. Wouldn't telling me this help her case?"

"She didn't want to accept any blame for your father's death, I guess," Matt said. "Even if she didn't order it, it happened because of her."

"I bet the investigator for the Magic Guild knew this, but covered it up, because he was into black magic, as well. I need to tell the Arch-Mage."

Missy hoped her car would survive yet another long trip back to San Marcos.

ARCH-MAGE BOB never took phone calls. At least not from someone as unimportant to him as Missy. She found him surfing, and she waited on the beach until he was done. He carried his mid-length board across the sand to where his Jeep was parked. He grabbed a towel from the back and dried himself off.

"Dude, what can I do for you?" he asked.

Missy told him what she had learned from the demon Asmodeus.

"Whoa, I can't believe you communicated with him. The Magic Guild forbids summoning demons."

"Yes, but I didn't summon him. You know that I'm strictly a white-magick witch. But I happen to know a former exorcist who's possessed by a demon. His demon spoke to Asmodeus. It was a demon-to-demon talk. No summoning involved."

"Way clever, dude. But, you know, I'm going to have to do something about your mother."

"Birth mother. Not the mother who brought me up."

"Yeah, I know," he waved away her correction. "She didn't summon the demon to murder your father, but that's what happened. And, like, she tried to kidnap you after we forbade her from keeping you. That means she's guilty. She's got to be held accountable, dude. Being banished isn't gonna cut it."

"You're not going to kill her or anything, are you?"

"No way. If the Guild's council votes to, we're gonna neutralize her."

"What's that?"

"It's a magical procedure that strips away her powers. She

won't be able to do magic again, except the simplest potions any regular human could do."

"Wow." Missy believed her mother deserved this, but she was taken aback by the idea. As a witch herself, she knew how devastating that would be. It would be like taking away an artist's ability to draw.

"Ophelia Lawthorne, or Ruth Bent, or whatever name she goes by, has been trouble ever since we banished her. She's constantly doing evil magic for her clients. You know this, dude. You've almost been killed by her."

"Yeah. You're right."

"Hey, if she wants to do magic again, she'll have to learn white magick. Start over from scratch and develop new powers, except for good, not for evil. She's got magic in her blood. We're not taking that away."

Bob pulled a T-shirt over his wide shoulders and beer belly.

"How do you do a neutralization?" Missy asked.

"Get her in a room with five magicians who simultaneously perform the spell. It's sort of like an exorcism, without the spinning heads and barfing."

Missy shuddered. "Good luck trying to catch her."

"Remember Jack, the ogre who tracked her down before?"

Missy nodded.

"He wants revenge for what she did to him. This time, though, he'll bring the cavalry with him."

19

JACK IS BACK

Jack the Ogre knew where Ruth Bent lived. The sorceress, who was really Ophelia Lawthorne, had a decrepit brick home in the woods of North-Central Florida. Jack had tracked her there, but he was captured with her magic and kept as a zombie-like slave until Missy Mindle freed him.

It had been humiliating, having to do her yard work and give her foot massages. He cringed at the thought of her groaning in pleasure, puffing on a cigarette, while he knelt on the floor, rubbing her smelly old feet.

A short scouting trip told him she wasn't staying at home. That would have been stupid of her to allow herself to be so easily found. She was hiding out somewhere while waiting for her kidnap victims to yield a usable kidney. Or two.

Missy had given him the location of the macabre operating room in the former orange-packing warehouse. It was a little over one hundred miles southwest of San Marcos, not in the same county, but awfully close to the territory she had been banned from.

Plenty of Bent's black magic still lingered on the property.

Jack sniffed the magic extensively. Ogres are like supernatural bloodhounds. No other creature smells magic as well as an ogre can. Or so Jack claimed.

In the back of the warehouse, out of view of the rest of his team waiting in the van, he stripped off his cheap sport coat and slacks. Then he performed a magic ritual Arch-Mage Bob had taught him that borrowed some elements from a Spanish Inquisition witch-hunting ceremony. Ogres have only a small amount of magic, but, combined with this spell and a few drops of his blood, it gave him a psychic link to the black magic he had scented here.

His olfactory glands created a target of the scent. It wasn't sulfur or brimstone. It was more like boiled cabbage. And unwashed sorceress feet. He shuddered at the memory of the foot massages. It was time to get his revenge.

He dressed and returned to the van. Inside was what Bob called "the cavalry," but was more accurately described as a ragtag crew of magic ne'er-do-wells.

Burt was an ogre, not too bright, but absolutely ruthless. Like Jack, he was a tracker/enforcer for the Magic Guild. Jessie was a Sin Eater, practicing a traditional magic from folk tales in which she took away the sins of mortal humans so they wouldn't go to Hell. This ability was also handy in taking the evil out of black magic. Tim, an elderly wizard, rounded out the team. Tim was meaner than a rattlesnake and the worst possible travelling companion. But his magic was powerful, specializing in combating black magic.

The two ogres were the muscle. The two others were the

magic. This time, Jack wouldn't be a sitting duck when Ruth Bent, aka Ophelia Lawthorne, blasted him with her sorcery.

Jack drove through the dirty lot to the edge of the two-lane rural road. He opened the window and sniffed.

The boiled-cabbage and smelly-foot scent came in a tiny burst floating in the wind. It came from the north. They rolled northward, Jack driving with his head half out of the window like a dog. The more frequent the bursts of scent came, the closer his target was.

They drove for thirty-five minutes until they came to a small town where another rural road bisected the one they were on. He sniffed heavily, then turned onto the other road leading east. Twenty minutes later, they approached the overpass of the interstate highway. On the right was a chain motel.

The scent-bursts were overpowering now. He pulled into the motel's parking lot. This was where the black-magic sorceress was staying. The ragtag team piled out of the van.

Jack pulled a crowbar from the rear of the van to wrench open Lawthorne's door. The motel's manager could call the police on them, but they would be gone before any cop arrived.

He had parked in a discrete spot behind the building next to the dumpster. As they walked around the side of the building toward the entrance, Jack stopped in his tracks.

He hadn't expected Lawthorne to be lounging at the pool. But there she was, lying on a chair, chain-smoking cigarettes, and using an empty beer car as an ashtray. She drank from a fresh can of beer and glanced at a magazine.

Two small kids, wearing floats on their arms, jumped in and out of the pool, running around screaming. Lawthorne fixed them with a baleful stare.

The two kids rose in the air, flew over the pool, and landed in the lap of their mother, who had been too busy scrolling on her phone.

Lawthorne returned her attention to the magazine.

"Okay," Jack said. "You guys know what do to."

Jessie spread her arms and began eating the evil. There was plenty to consume. Tim set about launching magic attacks. And the two ogres waited for the moment to snatch their prey.

The first spell Tim cast froze the mother and her two kids. They sat there like chubby mannequins, safely out of the way. He immediately followed by lobbing softball-sized glowing balls at Lawthorne.

She dove to the pool deck, trying to hide behind her lounge chair. A black-magic spell hit Jack's team, making Jack feel sleepy. But Tim had already protected them with a warding spell, so Lawthorne's effort was minimized. Tim continued lobbing the balls of magic, trying to disable his opponent.

"Good job, Jessie," the wizard said. "You've almost drained her."

It was rare for the mean wizard to give a compliment.

By draining Lawthorne of evil, it deprived her of the key ingredient to her black magic. Without it, she needed the assistance of supernatural creatures like demons. And there was no time to summon them.

"Go away! Leave me alone!" Lawthorne shouted as she crouched behind the chair, getting pounded with Tim's magic. "It's not fair. I did nothing to you."

"By the authority of the Magic Guild of San Marcos, we're putting you out of business," Jack said.

Ophelia's counterattacks had stopped completely. Tim cast a spell that made all her muscles go limp except those that controlled her vital functions. And the brief battle was won.

Jack walked through the gate into the pool area, picked up Ophelia, and threw her over his shoulder. It turned out he didn't need any extra muscle to bring her in.

Just extra magic.

MISSY RECEIVED the phone call from Arch-Mage Bob, while Darla was serving wine and cheese to guests at the Esperanza Inn.

"Hey, I thought I should let you know, like because you're family, that we got her," Bob said. "We're going to do the neutralization tonight."

"I want to be there," Missy said.

"Wow. Are you sure? It's not a lot of fun to watch."

"I'm not there to take pleasure in her punishment. I want to be there because it feels like the right thing to do."

"Cool. I get it. You're not a Guild member, but I guess you can come because of your relationship. You need to come with a member, though. The location is secret. I'll have Wendall drive you there, but you'll have to wear a blindfold before you arrive. Are you okay with that?"

"It's kind of weird, but I'm okay."

"Righteous. Wendall will pick you up around eight-ish tonight."

"Thank you."

Missy told Darla what was going to happen to Ophelia. "Do you think your mother should know, since she's her sister?"

"I'll let her know after it's done," Darla said. "Are you sure you want to do this?"

"Yes. It's the only way I'll feel closure."

Missy made sure to be waiting outside the inn before 8:00 p.m. She didn't know when Wendall would arrive, since the travel time to the secret location wasn't known to her.

She stood on the sidewalk outside of the inn in the balmy night air. It smelled of saltwater from the nearby bay, laced with garlic from a corner restaurant. Even though it was a pleasant evening, she felt dread. Her mother was going to endure an awful experience, and it was Missy's fault. No, make that her own fault. Missy was simply bringing the justice that had been long denied.

A giant Cadillac pulled up. The passenger window rolled down to reveal Wendall leaning toward her.

"Hop in. Your taxi is here."

She slid into the leather seat.

"Thanks for picking me up," she said.

"My pleasure. I'm glad to. Gives me time to discuss more of what you found out."

"Bob said I have to wear a blindfold?"

"Yep. But not until we get out of downtown."

"Okay. Thank you for allowing a non-member to go to your Guild Hall."

"It's not our Guild Hall. It's one of our facilities we use for, er, special occasions like this."

They were silent until they crossed Flounder Creek.

"Time to put the blindfold on." Wendall handed her a black linen hood.

She pulled it on, covering her entire head. The claustrophobia was instant.

"You know, I've been a Guild member for most of my adult life," Wendall said. "Joined just before I was thirty. I was a successful lawyer, married, with a small child. I'd dabbled with magic since college, and it was just a game to me. But when I was only thirty, my legal career just barely begun, I already knew something was missing."

He paused. Missy didn't say anything. She felt too claustrophobic to waste her breath saying something that would barely pass through the heavy hood.

"Regular human life—making money, buying bigger homes, becoming a partner in the firm, maybe going into politics— seemed so empty to me. Because I had tasted magic. Just a taste, mind you. But it showed me a whole other world was out there."

The car jolted as they went over railroad tracks. Missy had no idea where they were.

"Then I met Tommy. Tommy Albinoni. He was a forensic accountant our firm frequently hired. We had drinks one night, and the topic of magic came up. He'd sampled a taste of it, too. A deep drink of it, in fact. He was hooked, and what he told me convinced me to learn more. He taught me a lot of nifty stuff. And some scary stuff. He introduced me to other witches and wizards. This other world I had only glimpsed kept getting larger and larger. And more fascinating. More addicting."

The car stopped at a light or stop sign, then resumed.

"I went on to study with a master wizard. And mind you, this was while I worked twelve-hour days at the law firm and had a family and a home. But I finally achieved accreditation and joined the Magic Guild.

"You're probably wondering what I did with my magic," he continued. "Did I use it to help me in my day job? Oh, a bit here and there. But I was a corporate lawyer, not a defense lawyer. I didn't need to perform miracles."

He chuckled.

"Well, that's how I got into magic. It was a passion that gave my life meaning. Nothing more."

The car stopped again. Then Missy felt the vibrations of a dirt road beneath the tires.

"My wife got sick. My son was grown and off in Dallas, living his own life. It was just me and Becky. She was diagnosed with stage-four leukemia. That's when I turned to magic to help me."

Missy was worried about where this was going.

"I knew there was powerful magic that could heal cancer and other serious diseases. But no one in San Marcos seemed to know it. I was at the darkest level of despair. Until Louis let me in on a secret. He and some members of the Guild had been experimenting with black magic. They'd been looking for extremely powerful stuff, and black magic was where they found it. Black magic offered a cure to save Becky."

Missy finally interrupted.

"Black magic doesn't heal. My mother can't heal her kidneys with it."

"No, it doesn't heal," Wendall said. "It turned back the clock to before she was sick. It altered the time-matter continuum. Sure, we had to sell our souls to use it. But it worked. Becky suddenly went into remission. My hopes and prayers were answered."

Oh, my, Missy thought. This was truly distressing to hear this man she so respected had taken the dark path.

"Of course, my wife was taken by the cancer five years later. And all of us who tried black magic were under the spotlight. Your mother was banished. Tommy was caught and had to repent."

He cleared his throat.

"You understand, you weren't supposed to be able to read all the entries in the record books I showed you. The sensitive parts were encrypted by magic. I was shocked you had a spell to decipher them."

The encryption on the books was weak and sloppy, as if it had been done as a mere formality. Missy hadn't thought twice about decrypting them with a bit of magick.

"So, I never thought it would come to this, Missy. You're a good witch and a good woman. But we can't allow the integrity of the Guild to be destroyed by word of this getting out. It would destroy poor Tommy, so near the end of his life. And me, I was the one who assigned him to investigate your mother. Of course, Tommy whitewashed it all. He had no choice. To find her guilty would bring all of us down. Bring the entire Guild down, too."

"What are you trying to say?" Missy said in a muffled voice.

"I know you haven't mentioned anything about Tommy to Bob yet. And I won't let you do so. I'm sorry it must be this way. I need to protect us in the twilight years of our lives. And protect the Guild."

Missy grabbed the door handle. It was locked and sealed with magic.

A REPUTATION OF INTEGRITY

Missy pulled the hood from her head. No need for it now, once she realized they weren't going to the Guild's secret facility. She inhaled deeply, finally free of the stifling cloth.

Yet unable to flee this old wizard who intended to kill her.

Wendall placed a binding spell on her immediately after she yanked the hood off. An unseen force pulled her arms to her sides and her hands to her thighs. Her legs clamped together. Her head was the only part of her that could move.

The car drove down a country road in total darkness. There were no streetlights and very little moonlight. The road was flanked by thick forests that gave way to fields and pastureland. Occasionally, a front porch light shone from houses set far back from the road. And then the road would be swallowed by trees again.

"You don't have to kill me, Wendall," she said in the calmest voice she could muster. "I won't tell Bob about you and Tommy and Eliza-May. I really don't care about what you guys were doing over forty years ago. I only wanted to know who killed my father. Now that I have my answer, I couldn't care less about the Magic Guild."

"You don't understand how important it is for us to have a reputation of integrity," Wendall said, as if he were explaining to a child. "When you spend your life studying ancient traditions, and then you near the end of your life, you realize the only thing that will live on are the traditions you created. And the reputation you've built."

"Who cares if you played around in black magic?"

"I didn't play around. I sold my soul to keep Becky alive. Now, I have an enormous debt to pay in Hell. The reputation I leave behind on earth is all that keeps me from utter despair."

"But— "

"You're not listening." It was the first time she had ever heard Wendall's voice grow angry. "By practicing black magic, we betrayed the gift of true magic. You're a nurse. It's as if you turned your purpose to deliberately killing patients. Would you say that's not a big deal? That you could return to being a proper nurse and no one would care?"

"Don't compare murder to what you did. You didn't kill anyone. And you don't need to tonight."

"You're wrong. I have killed a few innocent individuals. And I'll do it again tonight. Don't worry. I'll make it painless. As long as you don't fight me, you won't suffer."

Missy didn't answer. She needed to concentrate on magic to defeat the binding spell.

Her hopes sank as she probed the energies around her in the car. Aside from the binding spell, the heaviness of other magic hung in the air. She couldn't tell what spells they were, but it was clear that Wendall had backups in case she broke the magic binding.

He was officially retired as a wizard. But this man still knew his stuff. No longer in his prime, he was nevertheless a more powerful magician than her.

They rode in silence. A yellow light appeared ahead, and Wendall pulled over into the entrance to a park of some sort.

A sign said, "Lake Paul State Park." Locked gate arms blocked the entrance. Wendall waved a hand. The padlock dropped from the gate, and the arms swung open inward.

Missy could have done that, too, with her magick. But it would have taken a lot more time and effort.

Wendall drove the car along a winding dirt road through the darkened park, passing picnic tables and trail heads. They went through a parking lot and then pulled up to a boat launch: two concrete ramps sloping into the water with a wooden dock in between.

"Are you going to drown me?" Missy asked in panic.

"You're going to drown yourself. It will look like suicide. But don't worry, I promise you won't suffer."

Missy tried creating a sleeping spell to disable Wendall. Halfway through the process, it simply fell apart. Wendall's magic defenses were too strong and extensive.

As a practitioner of white magick, Missy had always concentrated on spells of healing or protection, not offensive spells for attacking. She desperately searched her mind for something that could stop Wendall.

He climbed from the driver's seat. As he closed the door behind him, Missy made a thrust of power. The door snapped back open and hit the old man, knocking him backwards onto the dirt.

She tried to free herself, but the binding spell held.

"I won't blame you for trying your best," Wendall said, as he stood up and brushed off his pants.

He closed the door again and walked around the front of the car.

Missy released the parking brake and rolled the car forward. But not quickly enough. Wendall easily got out of the way. With her hands bound to her thighs, she couldn't touch the power charm in her pocket. Yes, it touched her leg through the fabric, but she couldn't get enough extra energy to propel the car more quickly. Plus, Wendall's magic hung over her like a cloak, stymieing everything she tried to do.

The car continued rolling and was finally picking up speed. Unfortunately, it was headed for the boat ramp, and she couldn't free the locked steering wheel fast enough to prevent the car from going into the lake with her trapped inside.

Defeated, she reengaged the parking brake.

"I admire your spirit," Wendall said, walking up to her door and opening it. "Come along now. Let's get this over with."

He intoned silent words and waved his hands over her.

An inexorable force took control of her muscles, moving her legs from the car, and forcing her body upright. Her arms still bound to her side, she marched awkwardly toward the water like a zombie.

"It was nice knowing you, Missy. May you rest in peace."

Suddenly, her heart stopped racing, and her adrenaline faded. She no longer was in absolute panic. This calmness wasn't her doing. Wendall controlled it.

She lurched toward the water. Her running shoes filled with water. It was cool, not cold. Then her ankles became immersed as she slowly descended the ramp.

But she wasn't frightened at all. Whatever Wendall had done to her mind made her look forward to being fully immersed, to breathe the water into her lungs in the peaceful depths of the lake.

As her knees went under, she almost slipped on some algae. But the force that controlled her kept her upright and marching along.

The water rose to her waist. To her chest. Then the ramp ended, and she dropped.

When her head went under, a vestigial part of her survival instincts took over. She held her breath. And she made one last, desperate attempt to save herself.

She sensed a living creature nearby. The bulk of a large alligator lying on the bottom of the lake.

She probed its primitive lizard brain. And commanded it to rise.

Something solid pressed up against the soles of her feet as she floated in the water. It was the alligator's back. As it rose slowly, she stood upon it until it pushed her high enough that her head crested the surface.

She turned her head with difficulty. Hidden in the dock's shadow, she believed Wendall couldn't see her. He stood, staring sadly at the lake. If he wanted to watch her die, he surely had the magic to do so, but hopefully, he didn't want to.

Her limited control of the gator felt unsteady. She didn't have enough power to maintain it much longer, and she was still paralyzed by the binding spell.

Ronnie, she cried in her mind, *help me, please.*

She repeated it over and over. Maybe the fact she was psychically connected now with the alligator helped, because he quickly answered, *How can I help?*

I'm being drowned in a lake by a wizard gone bad. I'm standing on the back of an alligator, but I can't control it much longer. And the wizard still has me trapped in a binding spell. Please get me out of this mess. See through my eyes. Hear through my ears. Please help.

The gator beneath her feet rose closer to the surface and moved toward the dock. She allowed herself to fall off and land atop the planks.

Wendall had turned around and begun walking back to his car. He must have figured she was a done deed by now.

His hearing wasn't too good at his age. The scraping sounds of claws and armored tails on the concrete didn't make him look behind him.

The nine alligators, big ones, moved quickly up both boat ramps on either side of the dock where Missy lay. She was surprised how fast they ran. And how tactical they were in their lizard brains, circling around to the right and left in a pincer movement to cut him off from his car.

Missy didn't know what kind of spell Wendall would have to fight off alligators. Because he didn't have the chance to use one.

He only had time to emit a small scream, more like a squeal.

Missy regained use of her limbs shortly thereafter. But she stayed where she was. She didn't want to attract the gators' attention while they were in feeding mode.

Wendall had seemed like such a kindly old man, a sweet grandfatherly type. And he'd been a fabled wizard. It was a shame he'd gone down the evil path, even if he had tried to correct his course afterwards. He'd made the kind of short-sighted decisions so many of us make, even the non-magical among us, when we choose to bend the rules or turn our backs on goodness to embrace the convenient advantage of the more powerful.

Missy had to wait for an hour for all the alligators to return finally to the lake and disappear below the surface.

Thank you, Ronnie, she said.

Wendall had left the car keys in the ignition, so she didn't have to remove them from a pocket of what was left of his jeans. She could have driven in his car back to San Marcos, but that would have been bending the rules and taking the easy way out. Instead, she stayed in the park and called 911 about a failed kidnapping that went terribly wrong for the kidnapper.

The next day, she found Bob in the office of his surf shop.

"Whoa, that is so jacked up," he said after she told him everything she knew about Wendall, Tommy Albinoni, and Eliza-May.

"I never would have thought Wendall had taken the dark path," he said.

"I'm so disappointed in him. Not just for that, but for trying to kill me."

"Yeah, that would be a bummer. But I guess he got the punishment he deserved. Dude, *gators*! I wouldn't want to die that way."

"It was fast. He didn't suffer for long."

Bob closed his eyes and shuddered.

"Tell me how it went with my mother," she said.

"Kinda like I told you it would. Like an exorcism with all the screaming and cursing. She's neutralized now. Won't cause trouble for anyone anymore."

"Is she okay?"

"No one hurt her."

"I mean mentally?"

"That chick never was right in the head in my book. She's not a happy camper right now, that's for sure. But my crew returned her to her motel all in one piece. Do you want to visit her?"

"No," Missy said. "I can't face her right now. I've got some thinking to do."

Two weeks later, Missy did see her birth mother. It turned out she came to visit Missy. Unannounced, of course.

SPECIAL TREATMENT

"Ruth?" Missy said after she answered the doorbell.

"Call me by my real name from now on. Are you going to let me in or not?"

"Yes, of course. Come in. You're not here to kill me, are you?"

"No. My magic's gone," Ophelia said, choking back tears. "I'm just the shell of the person I used to be. No longer a deadly sorceress. Just an old lady."

"I don't miss the deadly part," Missy said, leading her guest into the living room and pointing to the most comfortable chair. "Can I get you some water or tea?"

"Get me a beer and get it quick."

Missy hurried into the kitchen. She always kept some of the beers Matt enjoyed in her fridge, so she opened a bottle and popped her head in the living room.

"Do you want it in the bottle or a glass?"

"A bottle, not a can? Aren't we fancy? I never drink beer out of a glass unless it's from a keg. Just give me the bottle."

Missy complied. She tried not to stare, but she was shocked how her mother had aged since she last saw her. She looked weak and shrunken. White roots showed in her black-dyed hair. She sat sagging in the chair, defeated by life. Was it her loss of magic, her kidney disease, or both?

"Are you well, Ophelia?"

"Do I look well? No, I'm not. I'm at death's door. I need a kidney soon."

"Is that why you're here?"

"Stealing organs from society's voiceless hasn't worked very well for me."

Missy had evolved closer to deciding to give her mother a kidney. But then, she found another solution that, if it worked, would be better than surgery for both of them and less risky for a person of Ophelia's age and health. And it would free Ophelia from spending the rest of her life taking immunosuppressant drugs to prevent her body from rejecting the transplanted kidney.

"Would you consider a magick treatment to heal your existing kidneys?"

"Bah! No magic can do that."

"I know of some that I believe can. They're a combination of the tradition of earth magick that I follow plus secret spells of the native Timucuan people who once lived here."

"I want real American magic."

"Ophelia, they were the real Americans before the Spanish got here."

"Whatever. I tried everything I could. Before they took my magic away."

"You only knew black magic. That's not for healing. This magic is."

"I don't know."

"It can't hurt to try. And I mean that literally. Unlike black magic, this magic doesn't hurt people. And there's no demon to come after you if it loses its temper."

"I don't know."

"I want you to meet someone. Don Mateo, are you around?"

"Who are you talking to?"

"My ghost."

"You enslaved a ghost?"

"With white magic, you don't enslave other entities. He's attached to me willingly. Don Mateo, are you there?"

He appeared with an audible "pop" next to the television.

"At your service, Madame," the ghost said, giving a stately bow.

"Can you see him, Ophelia? Only people with magic in them can."

"Yes, I can see him. Even though they took away my magic."

"Don Mateo, this is my birth mother. Ophelia, meet Don Mateo. He was a very accomplished wizard in the early sixteen hundreds and fled to Florida to avoid the Spanish Inquisition. He compiled a grimoire of powerful spells that he developed in partnership with the shamans of the Timucuans. They include powerful healing spells."

Her mother seemed to pay more attention.

"What ails you, Madame?" he asked Ophelia.

"Why does he talk like that? It's kind of effeminate."

"That's how sophisticated people spoke during the seventeenth century," Missy said.

"Bah!"

"You're more ornery than ever, which means you still have some fight in you. You can beat this disease if the magic works."

"No one answered me about her ailment," Don Mateo said.

"Kidney failure."

"How horrible! I am pleased to say, however, that several elders of the tribe were cured with this spell." The ghost turned to Missy. "The 'Double Cypress Inveniam Viam.' It's in my addendum to the grimoire."

"You're just making that up," Ophelia said.

The ghost smiled. "Give us a chance, and we will demonstrate its effectiveness."

When Don Mateo said "we," he really meant Missy. Ghosts can't conjure magic. Some can do scary supernatural stuff, but they can't perform a spell step-by-step and harness the energies necessary to make it work.

Missy left her mother in the living room, watching TV, while she fetched the grimoire from its hiding place in the bottom of a kitty litter box. Next, she spent the next hour at her workbench in the garage using a mortar and pestle to grind herbs, seeds, and dried bird bones. She mixed in rare oils and a touch of water from the River Nile to make a poultice.

Her mother was glued to the television still when Missy passed through the living room to the kitchen. There, she drew a giant magic circle on the tiles and lit five candles around the circumference. She set the grimoire up on a recipe book stand just outside of the circle.

"Ophelia," she called. "Please come in the kitchen. We're ready for you."

Don Mateo hovered near the ceiling, just below the ceiling fan.

Moments later, Ophelia shuffled in, grumbling about how stupid it all was.

"Please come into the circle with me."

"You're doing it all wrong. Where's the inverted pentagram?"

"This isn't black magic. Just let me do my thing, okay?"

"Whatever. I'll play your silly little game if you insist."

"Sit down now!"

Ophelia plopped down on the floor next to Missy.

Now, Missy began the spell, gathering the energies within her spirit, from deep within the earth, the air, the water of the canal and sea outside, and the flames of the candles. Then she recited the words of the spell, a mix of Latin, Old Spanish, and Timucuan.

To achieve maximum power, she grasped the Red Dragon, the carved-metal talisman that was handed down from the ancient era.

Power buzzed in her hand, ran up her arm, and filled her solar plexus. Her entire body throbbed with powerful energy.

The lights in the house dimmed, and the bowl containing the poultice glowed as if it held embers.

"What the heck are you doing?" her mother complained when Missy spread the poultice on her mother's back, just beneath her rib cage, the closest point to her kidneys.

"It's burning!" Ophelia said.

Missy ignored her, remaining in the quasi-trance state.

The ointment glowed like lava on her mother's skin.

Missy shouted the final verse of the spell, and the power rushed from her body like a great wind. Her mother jerked as if hit by a heavy blow, her body convulsing.

Ophelia then collapsed on the floor in the fetal position and began snoring.

"*Fini*," Missy whispered. She, too, was about to collapse.

She wiped away a section of the circle's outline. And the spell was broken. Missy crawled from the circle and slumped against the kitchen island.

"Well done," Don Mateo said.

He drifted down from the ceiling and hovered above Ophelia. He ran his immaterial hands across the woman's torso, then he sniffed her. Ghosts shouldn't be able to sniff anything, but who wants to tell him that?

"I believe her kidneys are healed," he said. "You should summon a physician to bleed her with leeches to know for sure."

"I'll bring her to see a nephrologist tomorrow."

Missy sat there on the floor, too exhausted to move until the tea candles burned down and went out. Her mother continued to snore on the inside of the broken circle. Don Mateo eventually faded away.

"Thanks, Don Mateo."

Missy looked at the frail old woman she had hated since their first encounter. Could she ever learn to love this woman like she did the adoptive mother who raised her?

Nope.

But she would try to know her better and see how it went from there.

OVER THE NEXT TWO WEEKS, Ophelia underwent a series of tests of her kidney function. The nephrologist in Jellyfish Beach determined her kidneys were the healthiest he'd ever seen in a woman of her age.

Test results were sent to Ophelia's doctor near her home. Missy helped set her up on a video call with the doctor. Ophelia explained to him she'd had the tests down here because she was visiting her daughter.

"I didn't know you had a daughter," he said.

"Apparently, I do."

He said he simply couldn't believe the results.

"I've never heard of kidneys in the state of failure yours were in recovering like this."

Of course, Missy and Ophelia couldn't explain that magic was involved.

Ophelia said goodbye so she could return home and endure many of the same tests again under her doctor's supervision. They hadn't bonded much, since Ophelia had spent all her waking hours in front of the TV drinking beer or out on the porch smoking. Still, Missy felt a little closer to her.

"Next time I see you, I'll share some secrets about our family no one alive knows but me."

"Next time?"

"Yes. When you give me expensive gifts for my birthday."

"Gotcha."

Ophelia thanked Missy genuinely for her help and for the magic. Before she got into her car, she gave Missy the closest semblance to a sign of affection ever: an air kiss. It was better than nothing.

After her mother's car disappeared down the street, Missy petted her cats who had been terrified of the old ex-sorceress.

"You guys wouldn't know how many times I thought I'd have to kill that old bird one way or another."

The cats mrrred in agreement.

"I know you. You would never kill her," Don Matteo's voice said, though he remained unseen.

"Why do you say that? I'm not an angel. I've staked vampires before."

"Yes, you have," Don Mateo said. "But no vampire in the history of this planet has ever been as terrifying as that woman."

22

VAMPIRES DON'T ENJOY SUNRISES

After Missy's last patient visit of the night at Squid Tower, she walked to the end of the boardwalk that crossed the dunes and sat down on a bench.

Dawn would come soon. An almost imperceptible lightening of the sky above the ocean began. She leaned back against the wooden backrest and breathed in the salty air. It seemed all the drama of recent weeks had played out, and it was finally time to relax. Her mother would survive, and Missy still had both kidneys. The secret existence of the vampires, werewolves, dragons, and other supernatural creatures would not be revealed to the human world.

Most important, she was still alive and not a drowned body on the bottom of Lake Paul.

It was good to be alive. Literally. And she was happy to be alive in Florida where, on most mornings like this, she could sit by the ocean year-round and not freeze her butt off.

It would be nice to live on the ocean, she thought. Too bad it was impossible for a home health nurse to afford it. She wondered how vampire Detective Affird would afford to move to Squid Tower. Retired cops received generous pensions, though, she'd heard.

The sunrise began gradually, with a glow of purple that became orange. Low clouds were in the Eastern sky, blocking the sun's triumphal entry into the world, but making a fantastic image of contrasting colors.

Once the sun's disc broke the horizon, the sunrise accelerated. The clouds broke apart, and the sun appeared in all its glory above the ocean, with a reflection running atop its surface, like the Yellow Brick Road, straight to Missy.

Vampires could live forever. But they couldn't enjoy sunrises like this.

Now that the view of the ocean was bright enough to require sunglasses, Missy wearily stood and trudged along the boardwalk toward the building. She looked forward to sleeping all day.

Movement caught her eye at Squid Tower. Someone was on their balcony.

That was impossible. Any resident would be sun-torched at this time of day. It must be a repairman.

But as Missy got closer to the building, she got a better view of the occupant of the balcony.

It was Marvin.

No doubt about it. Marvin was moving about, looking for something on the balcony.

Marvin who was supposed to be dead.

Marvin, whom she thought she'd seen at MegaMart.

She raced inside the building and took the elevator to the Fourth Floor.

When the doors opened, she ran to 409. The door was locked. She rang the bell, then knocked loudly.

No one answered. Marvin didn't want to be discovered, naturally.

She knocked again, more loudly.

Or had she been mistaken? It wasn't Marvin she saw; it was a contractor. Or she had counted floors wrong, and the person she'd seen was on another floor. Perhaps, she had hallucinated seeing anyone at all.

She pounded on the door again.

The door of 410 opened.

Ethel Simmonds peered out, a sleep mask pulled down around her neck, a sheen of skin cream on her pale, vampire skin.

"Stop all the banging," Ethel said. "It's enough to wake the dead. Why are you banging on Marvin's door?"

"I thought I saw him on his balcony."

"You young people and your drugs."

"I'm not young. I'm forty-three."

"Show some courtesy for those of us who need our sleep."

Ethel closed her door and clicked the deadbolt.

Missy considered getting the spare key to Marvin's condo from Agnes. Or maybe she should give up this wild goose chase.

The door flew open. A hand grabbed Missy by the shoulder and yanked her inside.

"WHY ARE YOU BOTHERING ME?" Marvin asked.

"You're supposed to be dead."

"I'm undead."

"No, you're not," Missy said. "I saw you on your balcony in the sunshine a few minutes ago."

The man looming over her was unquestionably Marvin, but there was something odd about him.

"I was in the shade."

"So, if you're alive, who was sun-torched on your balcony?"

"My cousin."

"You have a cousin who's a vampire?"

"Yeah. Mike from Pittsburgh. Great guy. What a shame about his passing."

Missy's spell had given her a strong indication the ashes had belonged to Marvin, but she hadn't been certain.

"Did you keep him locked up in the guest bedroom?" Missy asked. "You have a deadbolt on the outside of the bedroom door."

"That's because Mick sleepwalks."

"Mick? You said his name was Mike."

"Mick's his nickname."

"Something about this just isn't right. Where have you been since Mick or Mike was sun-torched?"

"I've been out of town. Taking care of business."

"Right."

Missy glanced around the apartment. A box of paper files sat near the front door. The computer hard drives were in the process of being loaded into another box.

"Why are you packing up all this stuff?" Missy demanded.

"I'm done with all this garbage. It's a waste of space."

"All your Reptilian research? That's your pride and joy, I thought."

Marvin blinked at her in befuddlement. He struggled to find an answer.

That's when Missy finally realized what was strange about his eyes. The irises and pupils were vertical instead of round.

She stepped backwards. Come to think about it, Marvin seemed taller than she remembered. His bald head towered above her more than it should have.

And his nose seemed off. Instead of the bulbous nose she remembered, this one was a bit flatter, the nostrils more like slits.

"You're not Marvin, are you?"

The man stared at her with his unnatural eyes.

He shook his head no. She had the most outlandish thought.

"You wouldn't happen to be from the Alpha Draconis star system, would you?"

The man nodded. Make that, the Reptilian nodded.

Marvin and Bill had been correct. Reptilians really existed and could shape-shift into human form. The two conspiratorial vampires only got it wrong when they thought dragons were the Reptilian aliens.

Missy quickly conjured up a protection spell around herself.

The Reptilian must have sensed it. "I will not harm you."

"Why did you kill Marvin?" she asked.

"It was an accident. All I wanted was to take away some sensitive digital images he had of my comrades. I kept him as a prisoner while I searched his data and refined my transformation into his likeness."

"Then you killed him so you could take over his identity?"

"I was going to impersonate him and make internet videos denouncing his theories about my race, saying I'd been mistaken, and Reptilians really didn't exist after all. I would destroy all his data. Finally, I would find some rich Hollywood actor to impersonate and rule the world with their evil cabal. I didn't mean to kill Marvin. Once all the videos spread of him denouncing his own research, his credibility would be ruined, so who cares if he made more videos about us? I locked him on the balcony to keep him out of my way. How was I supposed to know the sun would kill him? There aren't any videos about that on the internet."

Missy wasn't sure what to do. Should she trap the Reptilian with a binding spell and bring him before the HOA board, so they could punish him?

Or should she allow him to continue his work, tamping down the insidious conspiracy theory that caused people and vampires to lose their minds and create mayhem?

While she was trying to decide, the creature's human clothes dropped to the ground. The Reptilian had shape-shifted into its natural state: tall, bipedal, green with glistening scales, a face like a gecko's. It sprinted to the balcony door, yanked it open, and leaped over the railing.

She went to the balcony and saw the lizard person sprinting over the sand dunes, across the beach, and into the ocean.

Missy shook her head, then left the condo. If encountering a Reptilian was the only freaky experience she had today in Florida, she would consider herself lucky.

It was a rare evening out for Missy and Matt. Normally, her working nights and his working days complicated planning anything that resembled a proper date.

Breakfast was their most common meal together. These meetings happened after Missy got off work and before Matt headed for the newsroom. Occasionally, they'd have a quick dinner before Missy went to see patients. Rarely, did they have drinks or dinner when they both had no obligations afterwards. When they did, it was to discuss strategy in the middle of solving a mystery.

Missy preferred it this way. She hadn't wanted Matt to shift the events into romantic dates.

Now, though, she was more open to a bit of sugar after dessert.

Matt appeared to be as well. Tonight, he was wearing a sports coat. She'd never seen him in one before. He had even trimmed his beard and shaved around it.

And he selected a nice steak and seafood place on the Intracoastal Waterway. It wasn't the surfer dive bar he normally frequented.

Matt ordered an expensive bottle of Pomerol.

Missy raised her eyebrows. "Is this a special occasion?"

"Any occasion with you is special," he said with a grin.

"Good answer. Your years writing articles have paid off with the *bon mots*."

"I just thought we deserved to celebrate," he said. "The truce between humanoids and reptiles has held. Your mother's kidneys are working properly. You survived a murder attempt. It's a lot to celebrate. I wanted to buy you a greeting card, but they don't have any that cover those happy moments."

"They must have 'I'm so glad you weren't murdered' cards, don't they? Did you look in the 'Get Well Soon' section?"

"I did. We'll just have to supply our own trite sentiments." His face grew serious. "But please don't get yourself into danger like that again. I don't know what I'd do if I lost you."

Missy wasn't one for overdone emotion. She usually reverted to humor in situations like this. But she was still haunted by how close she had come to being drowned by a man she liked and trusted.

Matt seemed to realize it was time to change the subject.

"Are you and your mother on friendly terms now?" he asked.

"As friendly as she is capable of. She's a narcissistic, selfish woman with a strong streak of evil in her. Not someone you can get really close to. And I don't really want to. Mabel, my adoptive mother, is still alive. She raised me and is my true mother in my eyes. If I'm going to spend a holiday with a mother, it's going to be her."

"It can't be so bad to have two mothers. I have zero."

"I know. I'm sorry."

Matt lost his mother several years ago.

"I don't see Dad as often as I should," he said, "though I've tried to convince him to move down to Florida. If I ever get married someday, he'll want to be nearby."

He looked at her strangely.

Marriage was not something she wanted to discuss.

"So, how's your bullet wound?" she asked.

"My bullet wound? The dragon completely healed it. You know that."

"Yes. But sometimes people with healed wounds feel phantom pain. Or itching. Or something."

Matt's eyes showed he knew why she changed the subject.

"So," he said, his eyes pointed off at an angle as he searched for another topic, "is the Reptilian conspiracy finally tamped out at Squid Tower."

"I believe so. But you never know with these things."

She didn't want to tell him about encountering an actual Reptilian. She didn't want to tell anyone. Ever.

Time for another subject change.

"These oysters sure are good, aren't they?" she asked.

Matt smiled and nodded.

Dinner went by with the smallest of small talk. When the check arrived, Matt insisted on paying for it.

"But we always split the bill," Missy said.

"We're not going to tonight. I've got this."

"Why? I didn't do any favors for you. In fact, I should pick it up to pay you back for being seriously injured twice because of what I dragged you into. Besides being shot, you also received burns from the dragon fire."

"That was all part of our agreement. I'm buying dinner tonight, okay?"

"Are you trying to turn this into a date?"

"Hey, you're the one who proposed carnal activities."

"Ah, now the fancy dinner all makes sense," she said.

After Matt paid the bill, he suggested they walk out onto the dock built for diners who arrived by boat. Aside from small lights on the surface of the dock pointing toward the water, it was dark enough to get a magnificent view of the star-laden sky.

"Beautiful," Matt said.

"It is."

"No, I was talking about you."

"Thank you. But I don't fall for that mushy stuff. I'm a nurse. I used to work in the ICU where patients could die on me. Now, I take blood-pressure readings of ancient vampires. There's no mushiness in my life."

"You've built up a hard exterior," Matt said, "but you have a big heart."

They stood there silently for a long time. It was breezy, so the wind kept the restaurant noise from drifting their way. No boats passed by. It was just the two of them, the salt air, and the billions of stars.

Missy was getting cold from the wind. She wished Matt would put his arm around her.

And then, he did.

She nestled into the crook of his arm, where she felt warmer. And needed. And less alone.

She had absolutely no desire to make a snarky comment like she normally would do. She simply stood there and enjoyed the night and the arm around her.

"That big heart of yours . . ."

Matt didn't finish the sentence because his mouth was upon hers. The kiss was long and hot, and she didn't even mind the tickling from his beard. When he finally released her lips, he finished his sentence.

"That big heart of yours—I want it to fall for me. Someday, at least."

She didn't know what to say.

"I want to kiss you again, but I'm not going to take you up on your offer to be a friend with benefits. It would be fun, but I'm just a small-town boy with old-fashioned ideas."

"No, you're not!"

He laughed. "Right. I read that on one of the greeting cards. What I mean to say is, I don't want to end up in your bed before I'm in your heart. I'll continue to be your buddy and get into ridiculous situations with you as we chase monsters around. I won't moon about and make you feel uncomfortable. I'll just be regular Matt, until the day comes when you fall in love with me. Maybe you never will. But I'll live with it. I'll still be regular Matt."

He stepped back to face her, placing his hands on her shoulders.

"Regular Matt," he said, "who gets to kiss you."

He pulled her toward him and kissed her again, with less heat, more sweetness.

"Okay, Regular Matt," she said. "Sounds like a plan."

She had no intention of falling in love again. But, after seeing a Reptilian jump off a fourth-floor balcony and run into the ocean, she knew anything could happen.

THE END

MORE

GET A FREE E-BOOK

Sign up for my newsletter and get *Hangry as Hell*, a Freaky Florida novella, for free. If you join, you'll get news, fun articles, and lots of free book promotions, delivered only a couple of times a month. No spam at all, and you can unsubscribe at any time.

Sign up at wardparker.com

CHECK OUT MY NEW SERIES: The Memory Guild midlife paranormal mysteries.

Starting anew at midlife, with two marriages behind her, innkeeper Darla Chesswick returns to her hometown. There has always been a bit of the paranormal in her family, but now she discovers she has psychometry, too—the ability to read people's memories by touching objects they have touched. And in San Marcos, founded by the Spanish in Florida five centuries ago, there are plenty of memories. Many of them deadly. Learn more at wardparker.com

ENJOY THIS BOOK? PLEASE LEAVE A REVIEW

In the Amazon universe, the number of reviews readers leave can make or break a book. I would be very grateful if you could spend just a few minutes and write a fair and honest review. It can be as short or long as you wish. Just go to amazon.com, search for "gazillions of reptilians ward parker," and click the link for leaving reviews. Thanks!

OTHER BOOKS IN FREAKY FLORIDA

Have you read Book 1, *Snowbirds of Prey*?

Retirement is deadly.

Centuries-old vampires who play pickleball. Aging were-wolves who surf naked beneath the full moon. To survive, they must keep their identities secret, but all the dead humans popping up may spell their doom. Can Missy Mindle, midlife amateur witch, save them? Get *Snowbirds of Prey* at ward-parker.com

Or Book 2, *Invasive Species*?

Gators. Pythons. Iguanas.

Dragons?

Why not? It's Florida.

Missy, midlife amateur witch and nurse to elderly supernat-urals, has two problems. First, she found a young, injured dragon in the Everglades with a price on its head. Second, her vampire patient Schwartz has disappeared after getting caught by Customs with werewolf blood. (It's like Viagra for vampires. Don't ask.) Order *Invasive Species* today at wardparker.com

Or Book 3, *Fate Is a Witch?*

Missy Mindle has two mysteries to solve. First, who is making a series of dangerous magick attacks against her that appear to be tests of her growing witchy abilities? And who is stealing corpses from funeral homes in Jellyfish Beach? When an embalmer is murdered, one of Missy's patients, a werewolf, is arrested. Can she exonerate him? Oh, and don't forget the hordes of ghouls and Hemingway lookalikes. Who will stop them? Find out at wardparker.com

Or Book 4, *Gnome Coming?*

They're coming for you.

Can you really blame garden gnomes for having a grudge? They're displayed as kitschy jokes, wounded by weed whackers, peed on by dogs. After midlife witch, Missy Mindle, seriously bungles a spell, gnomes throughout Jellyfish Beach, Florida, are becoming possessed by an evil force and are exacting retribution. Missy has to undo the fast-spreading spell and stop the surge of "accidental" human deaths. The problem is, her regular job is home-health nurse for elderly supernaturals, and she also has to help solve the murder of one of her werewolf patients. Like the gnomes, the Werewolf Women's Club is out for revenge.

And something is coming for her, too.

Get your copy at wardparker.com

Or Book 5, *Going Batty?*

A vampire tale even a caveman would love.

The retired vampires at Squid Tower in Jellyfish Beach, Florida, have it good. Until some ancient vampires show up. These strange bloodsuckers can turn into bats, unlike modern vampires. And they're also a bunch of Neanderthals. No, really. Not all Neanderthals went extinct. Some went undead. And now, they want to rule all the vampires of Florida.

Missy Mindle, midlife witch and nurse to elderly supernaturals, uses her magick to help her vampire patients fight back. But when the Neanderthals start taking vampire hostages, and kidnap the daughter of Missy's cousin, get ready for a conflict of prehistoric proportions.

Don't miss it. Visit wardparker.com

Or Book 6, *Dirty Old Manatee*?

Is he a mer-manatee? A were-manatee? Or just a trouble magnet?

When midlife witch, Missy Mindle, rescues two ill sea cows, she discovers one of them is actually a human shifter, Seymour. While a marine animal rescue organization cares for his female mate, Missy is stuck with frisky Seymour to nurse back to health—much to the jealousy of her reporter friend, Matt.

When they learn the manatees were sickened by a rare chemical, Missy and Matt try to track down the polluter. The body count grows as they face a nefarious corporation, a demon, and—scariest of all—Missy's mother, putting Missy's magick to the ultimate test. Meanwhile, she discovers what life would have been like if she hadn't divorced years ago: living with a flabby, middle-aged guy who leaves the toilet seat up. Order it at wardparker.com

ABOUT THE AUTHOR

Ward is a Florida native and author of the Freaky Florida series, a romp through the Sunshine State with witches, vampires, werewolves, dragons, and other bizarre, mythical creatures such as #FloridaMan. His newest series is the Memory Guild midlife paranormal mysteries. He also pens the Zeke Adams Series of Florida-noir mysteries and The Teratologist Series of historical supernatural thrillers. Connect with him on social media: Twitter (@wardparker), Facebook (wardparkerauthor), BookBub, Goodreads, or wardparker.com

ALSO BY WARD PARKER

The Zeke Adams Florida-noir mystery series. You can buy *Pariah* and *Fur* on Amazon or wardparker.com

The Teratologist series of historical paranormal thrillers. Buy the first novel on Amazon or wardparker.com

"Gods and Reptiles," a Lovecraftian short story. Buy it on Amazon or wardparker.com

"The Power Doctor," a historical witchcraft short story. Get it on Amazon or wardparker.com

Made in United States
North Haven, CT
05 October 2023

42386580R00134